MEDALLION
of the
BLACK
HOUND

MEDALLION
of the
BLACK
HOUND

SHIRLEY ROUSSEAU MURPHY
with Welch Suggs

HARPER & ROW, PUBLISHERS, New York
Grand Rapids, Philadelphia, St. Louis, San Francisco,
London, Singapore, Sydney, Tokyo, Toronto

Medallion of the Black Hound
Copyright © 1989 by Shirley Rousseau Murphy and Welch Suggs
All rights reserved. No part of this book may be used or reproduced in any
manner whatsoever without written permission except in the case of brief
quotations embodied in critical articles and reviews. Printed in the United
States of America. For information address Harper and Row Junior Books,
10 East 53rd Street, New York, N.Y. 10022.
Typography by Joyce Hopkins
1 2 3 4 5 6 7 8 9 10
First Edition

Library of Congress Cataloging-in-Publication Data
Murphy, Shirley Rousseau.
    Medallion of the black hound.

    Summary: The power of the Medallion of the Black
Hound brings David into a world called Meryn where he
must join in the battle of good against evil.
    [1. Fantasy] I. Suggs, Welch. II. Title.
PZ7.M956Me 1989   [Fic]   88-35825
ISBN 0-06-024368-6
ISBN 0-06-024369-4 (lib. bdg.)

To Darby

—S.R.M.

To my inspirators, David McMath and Derek Richardson; to my mentors and teachers, Barbara Hull, Helen Waite, and Ian Rogers; and, most of all, to my Mama

—W.S.

MEDALLION
of the
BLACK
HOUND

Prelude

Dark riders galloped through the nights in ancient Celtic times, robbers cruel as demons, burning cottages, destroying crops, sickening beasts with their magic. Hot-eyed wolves ran with them, pale, blood-hungry creatures lunging and slashing, killing any who dared defy them.

One man defied them.

A powerful king, Finn Mac Cumhal defied them. And a skilled mage he was, and he hunted with a pack of true, good hounds led by a bitch named Tuiren. Black as night was Tuiren, a wise, swift hunter; and, like her master, she knew the ways of magic. When the dark riders attacked Finn Mac Cumhal's lady riding with her women at dusk, their wolves cruelly wounding her, Finn set out to kill them. He was led by Tuiren.

When Mac Cumhal's pack killed the wolves, the dark raiders went wild with rage. They vowed to destroy the Celtic king, his lady, and their three small sons.

Now Tuiren bore two pups as clever in magic as she. They could strike a man weak with fear, turn a strong warrior helpless as a baby. Cleverly they protected Mac Cumhal's queen and children from the vengeance of the dark band: Mac Cumhal's family thrived.

After long years, faithful Tuiren grew old and died. Weeping, the good king took up hammer and brazier and, forming a magical mold, he melted pure gold and poured it, and set into it black obsidian. And with ancient spells he placed within the gold Tuiren's released spirit and her powers. When the metal cooled, Mac Cumhal drew forth a gold medallion bearing black Tuiren's likeness, and bearing her spirit and her powers.

As each of the two younger hounds grew old in his turn and died, Mac Cumhal brought home the hound's freed spirit to live within its own medallion. Each hound could appear at its master's bidding, black and huge, striking horror into its enemies. Each hound could also bring visions that would discover foes in far places: but each only with the help of its master, for in all ways the hound was servant to the bearer. It was said that two medallions together had powers beyond vision making, though the knowledge of those powers is now lost.

To each of his sons Finn Mac Cumhal gave a medallion. Finn's two older sons were wise with their magic, and Tuiren and Bran guarded their masters well. But the youngest son lusted after dark ways. With his mage powers he twisted the will of Sceolan to killing and theft: Thus did one hound serve evil.

When Mac Cumhal discovered his son's cruel ways, his rage shook the palace. He tore the medallion from the young man and drove him from the land. But that night the jewel chest where Mac Cumhal placed the medallion disappeared from Finn's chambers, along with his trusted sword. Late that same night a raiding ship sank in high seas off the coast. It is told that the son drowned with it; surely that son was not seen again on Celtic shores.

Soon after, the oldest son left home to cross the seas and discover new lands. His heirs grew up far from the old world; his medallion passed to his sons and to their sons.

Left to rule with his father, the middle son vanished suddenly, a mystery never solved. When Finn Mac Cumhal died, the rule of the kingdom passed to a cousin: The magic of the three medallions was gone from their land. But the power of the medallions was not lost.

chapter 1

David snapped awake sweating and lunged at the clock radio, then lay back, his mind seething with dark dreams, with jagged mountains and black wings battering around him, and the faces of strangers crying out. It was the medallion that brought the dreams: The gold disc lay heavy on his chest. He flung it aside, and the heavy gold chain pulled tight across his throat. His father had never told him the medallion would make him dream—he had told him only of its other powers.

David pulled himself awake and stared out his window at the dawn. It was the day of the game. He couldn't play soccer like this—his head was too muzzy from the dreams; he'd fall over his feet, make his team lose. He dragged himself out of bed and stood before the mirror, trying to bring himself back into focus, get himself straight. From the mirror, the medallion blazed against his chest bright as a burning sun, the black hound, lean and snarling, racing across the heavy gold. The hound was the real power; the spirit of the black hound was the real power.

But why did it make him dream?

He was getting awake now, the dreams shrinking back into—where?

Into his imagination? Or into a real *place*? His sense of that other, dream world was too real; and this wasn't the first time he'd dreamed of it. Sometimes he saw a man, a powerful man lying asleep, his face turned away, his golden beard spread across a pillow. In his dream he would reach out to that still figure, not knowing why.

He shook his head, stared again at the medallion's reflection and his own, and went to brush his teeth.

Later in the locker room, suiting up, he couldn't get his mind on the game. Snatches from the dream kept thundering through his head. He pulled on his jersey, making sure the medallion was hidden, to avoid guys asking about it. He didn't know what would happen if someone tried to touch it. He hadn't had it long, only a few weeks. He'd been shocked when Dad gave him the medallion so soon; Dad hadn't gotten it from his own father until he was eighteen.

That day, Dad had seemed so strange. He'd been hurried, getting ready to catch his plane, but that wasn't all of it.

Dad was usually pretty noisy; a big, heavy-boned man, his light hair always mussed, his short beard well trimmed, his hard hugs and strength making David feel safe and right. But that day, when he'd dropped the gold chain around David's neck, he'd been too quiet, his green eyes solemn. David had felt the weight of the medallion and stared down at it filled with unease.

"Now? You're giving it to me now?"

"Before I go away. I want it safe. And I want you safe. Come on, we'll talk on the way." They had piled into the car, David pressed between his parents, and headed for the airport. It was an extraordinary thing for his father to be leaving his college classes in the middle of the semester.

Uncle Joe had called from England less than two hours earlier; a tense, anxious conversation. Joe wasn't sick or hurt, Dad just wanted to get over there. It was a long flight and an expensive one, but he hadn't hesitated. He had turned away from the phone looking wound up: a lot of controlled energy ready to burst out, the way he looked on the track when the teams were ready to run. Joe was Dad's half brother; they were very close. The diving crew Joe worked with was excavating a sunken Viking ship off the coast of Wales. Its discovery had been all over the papers:

Remains of twelfth-century Viking raider discovered . . .
Rare Celtic treasures found in Viking ship . . .
Ancient jewelry and coins brought up from Welsh dive . . .

Dad had been really excited when the ship was found. Besides his coaching, David's father taught medieval history. He was a scholar of Celtic literature and history, and was writing a book on it. But his interest in the dive was more than professional eagerness. As he cradled the phone, his face had been hard with controlled anger. "Balcher's on the diving crew—he's hired on."

Mom's eyes had darkened; she had reached to touch Dad's arm in a gesture of concern.

David knew Balcher had appeared at two other dives off the English coast, upsetting Uncle Joe with his strange, threatening behavior. Dad and Joe had been so concerned, they began to investigate him. They found he had an ugly prison record for extortion, and for some kind of terrorism. And then, because Balcher was of Celtic descent, Dad began to trace his family.

The old records and documents showed beyond doubt what Dad at first had been almost unwilling to believe: Balcher was heir to one of the three medallions. David had seen his picture, a completely bald man with a curiously small, slick head, with a scar across it like a snake.

They had completed the investigation a year ago. Dad had been edgy ever since, scanning several newspapers daily, two of them British, writing frequently to Joe. Dad and Joe were convinced that Balcher was searching for the lost medallion. The man hadn't stayed long at the earlier dives, as if he felt that they were not excavating the right ships. But it looked as if he meant to stay with this one.

Mom said, "Why did Joe let them hire him?"

"Joe isn't the boss," Dad said. "Balcher had references, and they needed hands."

David said, "Doesn't Balcher travel with two other men? Are they with him?"

"Not at the dive. But maybe ashore somewhere." His father had turned away, preoccupied with plane reservations and what to do about his classes. He and Mom had started making hurried plans, and David didn't ask anymore. The only plane reservation his father could get all week was less than two hours away; their rushed packing and many phone calls had been like a major fire drill. But just before they had piled into the car, Dad had removed the medallion from beneath his shirt and dropped the chain around David's neck. David didn't know what he felt—pride? excitement? a sudden heavy responsibility that wasn't comfortable.

Driving to the airport, Dad had talked about the medallion's ancient past, and about its power to bring the spirit of the hound. Four times in his life David's father had called the hound, each time to battle an evil that threatened more than himself. And there were other times when the hound had appeared without being called. One night, David and his folks had returned from a movie to find the house torn apart, televisions, cameras, silver piled by the door. When the cornered burglar came at Dad with a crowbar, the hound exploded between them, suddenly powerfully real, driving the man back, its eyes burning, its growl low, rumbling. Dad had held the white-faced burglar while the hound paced and threatened and Mom called the police; the hound was gone when they arrived. Before it vanished, David had reached to touch its broad, shaggy shoulder, had felt its warmth under his hand, its hard, powerful muscles, had smelled its scent, rank and wild. It had stared at him calmly, its eyes golden, deep. Then it had vanished.

The shouting in the locker room rolled around him. He pulled on his soccer shoes, thinking about the danger his father might be in somewhere on the seas off Wales.

Dad had been so excited about the ancient ship! Driving, watching the traffic, he had made David almost see the broken ship lying in the mud of the seafloor.

"She's on her side, pretty deep, the ribs smashed, the keel intact. They're already bringing up gold—weapons, tableware, jewelry. It was one of the raiding ships, all right, sacking the Celtic coast. The old tales say Mac Cumhal's son took part in those raids—stole from his own countrymen." He had turned to look at David. "They've brought up a gold-hilted sword embossed with a running hound."

David had caught his breath. "Mac Cumhal's coat of arms."

Dad nodded.

They had turned off the interstate to the airport, David touching the medallion with a strange, excited feeling. Dad had glanced down at him, his green eyes intense. "The medallion will never harm you. It will help if you are in danger, but only according to your need. The hound will come when there is need to protect *you*." Dad had paused, his jaw tight.

"But if you are to battle a larger evil, you must call the hound. And no one can touch the medallion, David, except one of the heirs to its power." Dad had given him a long look. "Use its power as you must to keep it safe—to keep yourself safe."

What did Dad think might happen?

Could the third medallion—if Balcher found it—track this medallion here?

The old tales said that two medallions together could bring further powers, but they did not say what. David had a sudden sense of the two medallions locked in some potent battle.

Dad said, "The medallion protected me in the war. It can't turn back bullets, but in combat it can strike terror into your enemy, make strong men lose their nerve. Pure fear can be a physical sensation as powerful as an electric shock." He was silent a moment; then: "Twice on the battlefield the black hound ran beside me, his eyes blazing like the fires of hell. To know him will weld you beyond question to the power of Mac Cumhal's legacy—to Finn Mac Cumhal's belief in right and justice." His father's look had been steady. "This power is never to be used lightly. It holds for its bearer a solemn commitment."

David had nodded, already weighted heavily with that commitment.

"If Balcher can, again, turn the power of the third medallion to evil, he could create terrible havoc in our world. He must be stopped."

As Dad pulled the car into the short-term

parking, David lifted the chain from around his neck. "Then you must wear it. You can't go there without it."

"No." Dad took the chain from him, put it back. "I don't want to have the medallion. As an heir to the medallions, Balcher would sense it.

"Balcher—from the reports I was able to get, Balcher is a true psychopath, a man without conscience. A psychopath doesn't feel fear like a normal man, sometimes feels no fear at all. Yet the greatest power of the hound is to strike a cold, debilitating fear into its enemies.

"And Balcher could be completely immune to that fear."

"But . . ."

"There are other ways to battle Balcher. Legal ways."

They had sat a minute looking at each other, David filled with fear for his father but silenced by his father's strong purpose. Then they snatched up suitcases and raced for the ticket counter, David's mind still whirling with questions.

In the airport, Dad had held Mom a long time, then hugged David tightly. David stood with his arm around Mom, watching his father board the plane.

The coach's whistle jerked him back; the shouting in the locker room registered again. He moved with the shoving, scuffling team out to the field, his ears filled with the coach's thunder and his teammates' boasts and laughter. His friend Derek yelled too loud, "Watch Camden—their left fullback—break your leg if he could . . ." and they got a look from the entire opposing team; the look from Camden was mean with promise.

The toss—the kickoff. David forgot the medallion in the fever of the game and wasn't aware of it again until someone kicked the ball out. In the pause for his team to take the throw, he realized the medallion was burning hot against him, so hot he grabbed it in a handful of shirt, jerking it away from his skin. What was wrong with it? A strange fear filled him. He stood holding the medallion in his clutched shirt, watching the field, the sun beating on his shoulders. Maybe it was the sun's heat making the gold disc burn. It cooled a little, he let go, but the fear did not let go. The shouting from the stands had turned into a muddle of conversation and a few little kids' giggles and screams. He looked up at the stands and found Mom, her dark short hair sticking out under her baseball cap. She gave him a thumbs-up, and he grinned back.

The throw-in was a poor toss, but a teammate managed to head the ball. David moved to receive a pass and relay it down the field. An opponent intercepted and kicked the ball in a high, fast trajectory down the field to his own forward, who had moved behind the defenders. The stands thundered, half with anger, half with cheers. David's team yelled for a call of offsides.

David stood sweating as his team took positions for the free kick. The medallion still burned, distracting him; then he realized it wasn't hot but sharply cold, like ice pressed against him. What was it doing? What was wrong with it? Get your mind on the game! He concentrated on the field boiling around him, received the next pass from a midfielder, and, back in control, dribbled the ball fast down the sideline, his heart pounding, sweat half blinding him as he slipped the ball past their inside forward.

Sidestepping, feinting and faking, he found a hole and moved the ball on, the stands shouting, *"Go, David! Shoot! Shoot!"* He avoided a midfielder coming at him; the smell of bruised grass came sharp. Camden was on his weak side. David dodged, drew Camden off balance, turning to pass. He saw the flash of Derek's earnest face, moving to receive; saw Camden's foot snake out to trip Derek. . . .

Derek flipped and crashed hard, sprawling; David heard the sound of bone snapping. Derek's face drained white; his arm was jammed back in an impossible position. David stared, not believing; he could feel Derek's pain and shock.

The ref's whistle was shrieking, *Foul! Foul!* The angry stands roared. The coach crouched over Derek. David was burning with hatred for Camden, wanting to kill the smirking creep— He spun, grabbed Camden . . .

Someone jerked him back.

"You can't kill the dude."

"Cool it, Dave."

"Get in—get him on the field. . . ."

A stretcher took Derek off the field, and play resumed. David got the ball and headed past Camden, glancing him with a sharp clip to his shoulder, a warning gesture. He made Camden twist sharply, stumbling away from the ball, and laughed at Camden's look of hatred as he pounded on, preparing to score. The medallion was freezing him; he drew back his foot to send the ball past the goalkeeper.

He didn't connect.

The ball wasn't there. The field was spinning, going foggy . . .

The field blurred and faded to nothing; his teammates faded, twisting away. He grabbed for the nearest player and hugged empty air, heard the stands shouting far away. He was falling through blackness, the field gone. . . .

Falling—spinning down through dark emptiness, careening and tilting down, the air pushing him down like giant hands—dropping . . . dropping him. . . . He yelled and was sucked down faster, screaming and knowing that nothing heard him. . . .

How long he fell he couldn't guess. He was covered with icy sweat, his soaked jersey frozen to him.

Had they all fallen? Was the whole field gone?

But he had seen them standing, thin as shadows as his own body was jerked and twisted; he had seen them staring, shocked, the field warping away like a sheet of rubber, then gone.

He could imagine his mother seeing him vanish, could feel her cold terror, could see her leaping up, running down the stands onto the field. . . .

His soccer shoes felt like lead, weighting him, dragging him down faster.

Suddenly a light flashed out of the blackness and sped past him; he reached toward it. Another came; the blackness was now smeared with lights. He clutched the air dizzy and pleading, reaching out to the lights like a baby reaching toward shapes and colors it didn't understand.

The lights slowed, began to come together, to form into groups. He could see color—brown, green . . .

Trees!

There were trees below him. He was falling fast toward them. He plunged into the branches.

They tore at him, jabbed him, and broke his fall. He hung tangled in the rough limbs, staring down at the ground far below.

This is a dream. I'll wake up.

Any minute I'm going to wake up.

The limbs he clung to were bright green, twisted and rough. The masses of leaves that blew around him were brown—alive browns, light filled, like new growth. The distant forest floor was green and rolling, and the woods smelled rank, stagnant. His heart was thudding like a motor racing off beat. His mother's worried face filled his mind.

Mom . . . get me out of here! What is this!

When he tried to free himself, the branch cracked and he fell again, grabbing for another limb, flinging his legs around it. He stopped himself with a jolt that cut his legs deeper. He hung there, breathing hard. Now he was mad, ready to hit something.

At last he climbed down, branch by branch. When he reached the bottom limb, it was still a long way to the ground. The trunk was too big to straddle. He dropped the last ten feet into the moss, hoping it was as soft as it looked. It gave, bouncing him like a mattress and belching out a putrid breath.

There was no sound. He stood up and looked around him, trying to swallow back terror. The whole forest seemed to be moving, the ground heaving like an ocean, making him dizzy. He felt that something was watching him, that something among the moving shadows was waiting to see what he would do.

chapter 2

He swiped at the blood running down his legs;
his socks were soaked with blood, and his white
shorts and jersey smeared green from the moss.
The wind turned his sweat clammy cold. The
hilly forest floor still swayed, making him feel
sick. But then he realized the movement was
only the blowing tree shadows racing across the
ground. Above him the sky was too dark a blue,
the sun not fierce as it had been over the soccer
field but dim and small, farther away.

This wasn't happening! This wasn't his world!
He felt as if this place, too, would vanish and
drop him again into nothing. Fists clenched, he
searched the sky's emptiness as if he might see
his own world hanging up there.

A dream! It's only a dream!

But it wasn't a dream. The wind, the musty

smell, the little, faraway sun—his stinging legs and dripping blood . . . Not a dream. He snatched at the medallion. It had done this, it had sucked him out of his own world to . . . *Where?*

Where was he?

Why had it done this?

Dad said the medallion's powers would protect him. Then why had it brought him here? The way it had burned him, hot then cold—what had it done to him? Had it, too, turned evil?

Yet twice since the day Dad gave it to him the hound *had* helped him.

The first time, he'd been alone in Mr. Rolf's classroom copying the assignment after late practice, when Mr. Rolf burst in suddenly, wanting to know what he was doing in there alone.

"I had to go to special practice this morning—I didn't get all the assignment."

"You should be quicker. I don't like you alone in my room." The man had a loose white face that was somehow deeply frightening. The kids stayed away from him when they could. "There's been another theft," he said coldly. "In Mrs. Blakken's room."

David had stared at him, furious. "I'm not stealing. I'm copying your assignment."

Mr. Rolf had pressed forward, backing David into the corner, a dark, ugly rage about him. He reached for David, David clutched at the medallion; the shadows had heaved and the hound was there, black and huge, its great shaggy body tensed to spring. The teacher's face had gone whiter; he had backed away, stumbling, had run, bursting out the door; David could hear him running down the deserted hall.

David had gotten home fast, slammed into his room, and stayed there until dinner. To have felt the hound's power as his own had changed forever something within him.

Mom would not disturb the privacy of his closed door, but when he came down to dinner she had that puzzled, caring look. David had slid in at the table, staring at Dad's empty chair. When he looked up at her, he knew he owed her an explanation for his long, silent afternoon. They had only each other now, without Dad. David had looked down at his plate, then up at her. He could say only, "School—Mr. Rolf."

"Oh," she said, her brown eyes searching his. "I don't like him either." There were questions in her eyes he didn't answer. She had let it drop; they had said nothing more about it.

The hound had come to him the second time while he was delivering papers. It was nearly dark when three tough boys from school skidded their bikes around him, threw him down, and scattered his papers. When they started to smash his ten-speeder, he piled into them, kicked two of them in places that made them double over. They kicked him hard; and suddenly the hound had leaped past him out of nowhere, snarling, spilling them across the pavement. He had felt power from the medallion that day, just as he felt it when he was jerked away from the soccer field.

He stood with his back to the tree, watching the swaying woods. His sweat-damp shirt was cold; he was painfully thirsty. He touched the medallion angrily, willing it to take him home.

Had there been some danger on the soccer field, was that why it had jerked him away?

Silent and furious, he commanded it to take him back. There were no spells, only his own will. When nothing happened, his anger turned to rage; he wanted to tear the medallion off and throw it as far as he could.

He kept watching the woods. Every shadow looked like something alive. The sound of the wind would hide the sound of footsteps. The tree trunks were so twisted that anything could be hiding behind their thick gnarls. He didn't like standing in one place. He began to walk, shifting among the trees, staring into the shadows and among the wind-tossed branches. When he looked behind him, his trail of deep footprints had begun to disappear, the moss springing up as if he had never passed. A twig snapped and he spun around, heart pounding.

He could see only the blowing shadows and wind-jerked branches. No, wait—where two bent trunks pushed together, something bright shone out.

An eye, watching him.

No, two eyes.

He stared until he could make out the face half hidden in shadow.

It looked almost human but it was as green as the trunks of the trees.

A green hand moved.

He wished he had a weapon. Better not run. If he confronted it, maybe it would back off. He found a fallen branch, hefted it, and moved toward the green creature. If it was dangerous, wouldn't the hound appear? The green face was hard to see clearly, all caught in blowing shadow. But its eyes shone steadily, then opened wider, with an intensity that chilled him. A predator's look?

Or a look of fear?

chapter 3

Shadows swam across the green face. The dark, watchful eyes didn't blink, only changed expression. Then the wind eased and the shadows stilled, and David could see the face clearly. It seemed very human, fine featured and framed with long, dark hair tangled across a curved cheek and a small chin.

A girl! It was a girl!

She slipped out from behind the trees and stood looking at him: a green girl, a sword gleaming in her green hand.

Her clothes were brown, splotched with green, like camouflage. She moved toward him silently, her dark eyes seeing everything about him. When she was very close, she reached to touch his cheek. As her arm stretched out of the leather sleeve, a pale line of normal pink skin showed.

Stain! She had smeared herself with green stain. The skin edging her eyes and inside her ears was as ordinary as his own.

They stood looking at each other with curiosity and caution, until suddenly a dull thudding struck the forest. Her eyes widened in alarm. She grabbed his wrist with a strong green hand and pulled him in between the trees.

A vine ladder hung down among the trunks. She shoved David at it. The thudding was coming closer. He climbed, and she came up fast behind him. He bellied off the ladder onto a platform high in the leaves, rolling out of her way.

She jerked the ladder up, and they crouched on the edge, looking down through the leaves. The thudding was accompanied now by grunts, then a rumbling shout. Suddenly five gigantic men appeared between the trees, covering the ground with huge strides, shaking their fists at one another, grunting and complaining and prodding. They were half as tall as the trees, broad as trucks, lumpy and humped, and dressed in ragged animal skins with the heads and feet dangling. They looked as if they could smash a human head with a casual slap. They carried thick spears that in a human hand would be too heavy to throw. They paused beneath the platform, arguing in thundering voices.

Soon they had trampled the smaller trail to nothing. They didn't look up, nor seem to see at their feet the already trampled moss. The girl winked at David and settled back on the platform against a leather pack, casually dismissing them. David studied the small, leaf-walled room.

The platform was made of straight saplings laced together, its floor covered with a mat of woven grass. The tree's own branches had been cut to raw stubs, pale among the heavy leaves. A leather hammock hung at one side. Overhead, hanging from limbs, were leather bags and a short saw.

The giants' voices rose, booming with rage; they were hitting and slapping one another. The girl looked down at them casually, as one of them yelled, *Ponies*, then *Fresh meat*, his accent thick and strange. The girl looked bored, had sheathed her sword, though her hand didn't move far from it.

"I am Jendovee," she whispered, leaning close. "You came out of nowhere. The wood was empty, then suddenly you were there in the tree. You have powerful magic. Who are you?" Her eyes were very dark brown, with a glint of humor about them.

She studied his stained soccer jersey, frowning at the black diagonal stripe and black letters. "Is that your name—MARAUDERS? She pronounced it oddly: ma-roo-dairs.

He stared down stupidly at his jersey.

"What is your name?" she whispered. "Can't you speak? Can't you understand me?" She unsheathed a small knife from her belt and began to write on a branch with its tip. *Jendyfi*, she wrote, and looked at him, puzzled.

"Jen-dov-ee," she said slowly again, watching him carefully. "I am Jen-dov-ee."

"David," he whispered. "I'm David. Of course I can speak. That's a funny way to spell Jen-dov-ee."

"That's the way it is spelled," she said, looking even more puzzled. She printed *Davyd*, then touched his bare, tanned arm and his white sleeve. "Magician or whatever you are, you would do well to stain yourself green. That white, and your bare skin, can be seen for miles." She kept looking at him, her frown filled with questions.

The shouting giants had worked themselves into a frenzy, hitting each other so hard the tree rocked with their lunges against it.

Jendyfi said, "All they do is fight. Good thing. That's what saved my hide."

"Why? Were they chasing you just now, down in the woods?"

"No. I came down to see what you were. But they—they chased me once." Her look went closed. He waited for her to go on, but she didn't. She seemed torn between wanting to talk and wanting to keep her privacy.

But then, after some time, she said, "They wrecked my cave. They wrecked everything in it that they couldn't eat. They were fighting over me when I slipped away." She didn't seem to want to say any more, but studied his stained jersey. "If Marauders isn't your name, is it your city? Your clan?"

"It's a soccer team."

"What's that?"

"A game. On a field." Did she know what a game field was? "It's—you kick the ball toward your opponent's goal."

"Oh, like pel-traws." She paused. "Or pel-tranc," she said darkly. "Is it like pel-tranc?"

"I don't know. What's pel-tranc?"

"If you don't make the goal, your life's forfeit."

"No, it isn't like that. You can't be serious. They kill you for missing a goal?"

"In the Undercity they do. But only their prisoners play it. The losing prisoners die." She parted the leaves to look down again at the giants. "They've come looking for the ponies— they can still smell them. I chased them away two days ago, but ogres have good noses; they love pony meat."

"I thought they were giants." He peered

through the branches. "Won't they smell *us*?"

"Ogres, giants, all the same. They won't smell us while the pony scent is there. They're too simpleminded to sort out anything very complicated. They never were much of a threat until the Degra did their dirty work on them. Now they're—Now you want to keep clear of them." There was fear deep in her eyes, behind the mask of boredom, as if perhaps she had lived with fear a long time.

"Who are the Degra?" David said.

She looked at him wide-eyed and didn't answer. He didn't repeat the question.

The ogres were shouting "Powoony" and "Freoosh meoot" at each other as they started away, crashing through the woods. When David looked back at Jendyfi, she was rummaging in one of the leather bags.

He said, "Do they eat people as well as ponies?"

She nodded, but avoided looking at him.

She pulled from the bag a leather tunic stained green, leather trousers marked with green, a dagger in a sheath, a belt, and some soft boots that laced up the sides. She handed him a crock filled with green paste that smelled like the forest moss. "You can't travel in those clothes."

"Travel?"

"They'll be back, now they have it in their heads about the ponies."

He stared at the clothes.

"Dress first," she said patiently, "then smear the paste on." She turned her back. Then, suddenly realizing something, she turned around again.

"You don't *want* to stay here? They'd kill you. They may be stupid, but they can be terrible when— You never know when the Degra will make them blood hungry. Where were you meaning to go?"

"I don't even know where I *am*. I don't know what place this is—what world this is." His terror rose again, a surge of helpless fear filling him, like something alive crawling inside.

She took his hand, and held tight until he calmed. "You are *not* from our world," she said softly, her eyes huge. "You know nothing about it." Her hand was warm and steadying. "You are in Cymru Forest. In Meryn. This world is Meryn. How—how did you come here? By what power?"

He started to reach for the medallion, but something stopped him. "I was playing soccer, about to kick a goal, then there was blackness and I was falling. I kept falling . . . I don't know why. . . . I couldn't see—just emptiness . . ."

Her brown eyes looked so deeply at him that he squirmed. Her lashes were dark and thick, her green-stained nose tilted—a nice nose. She was trying to understand, trying to know what the falling had been like. She said, "Get dressed, David. Do you have a last name?"

"Shepherd. David Shepherd." He took up the soft leathers, pulling them on over his shorts and jersey, then sat down on a branch to pull off his shoes.

The boots were too small. He put his soccer shoes back on and smeared them with the green paste, then covered his face and arms and hands with it.

He strapped on the knife, watching Jendyfi pack the rough iron saw into a leather bag with two blankets, some dried fruits and meat, and a leather bottle. Her quick, spare movements at the simple task made him think of his mother getting a meal, fast and easy, with no motion wasted. His mind filled again painfully with Mom looking for him, shouting for him, wild with panic.

Were they all searching for him? Both teams, the coach racing through the stands, shouting through the locker room? He was wrenched with emptiness, with need for the adults he trusted, with fear of the unknown, to be faced alone. He stared at Jendyfi, swallowing. He had only this girl—this girl no older than he—between him and total panic.

chapter 4

"The ogres will return," Jendyfi said, pushing back her dark hair. "They'll track the ponies, then come back where the scent's strongest, where the ponies stopped to graze. We'll go as soon as it's dark—we can lose them better then."

David wasn't wild about tramping the forest in the dark with ogres around. But he hadn't much choice; Jendyfi knew this world, he didn't. He wished he could close his eyes and open them on the soccer field in the hot sun, see the team . . .

He supposed Mom had called the police, that they'd be searching for him. He wondered what she'd told them—that he'd vanished into thin air? They'd call her a nut. No, she and the coaches would have made up something. But what about the team, the people in the stands?

Maybe his photograph was on TV. David Shepherd, son of Robert and Susan Shepherd of 2961 Royden Place, missing since Saturday afternoon, when he disappeared suddenly and mysteriously from the soccer field at Stevenson Gaming Center. Reports are garbled. Neither police nor reporters have been able to make sense of the incident. Coach Milner said . . .

He wondered if *time* was the same at home. Maybe time was frozen. Maybe there was no need to call the police, maybe everyone was still on the soccer field just after Derek was hurt, and he, David, held in that instant when he kicked to make a goal—maybe no one knew what had happened.

Or, if time was different, maybe he'd return to his own world like Rip Van Winkle, after everyone he knew and loved had grown old or died.

If he ever did return.

He looked at Jendyfi, suddenly very glad he wasn't completely alone. "Where was your cave? The cave the ogres attacked."

She pointed off through the woods. "In the white cliffs at the edge of the forest. You can't see them from here. I went there when they— when the ogres destroyed our home." She looked away, her face closed.

Then she looked back at him, suddenly letting

him see her pain, her dark eyes stricken. "They burned our house. They killed my parents. The Deg—" She bit her lip, looked down.

"The Degra made them?" he said softly.

She nodded. "I was driving the goats from pasture. We had the best goat herd in Meryn." She swallowed, then went on. "When I got home, the house was hot ashes and smoke. My parents, my little sisters . . ." She turned away from him, her fists pressed to her mouth. "The ogres' footprints were everywhere."

He put his arms around her. She was still as stone, trying to keep control. He held her until she let herself lean against him, let herself cry. He thought she hadn't had anyone to talk to, or to care about her, for a very long time. He held her tightly while she sobbed.

Crying girls made some guys uncomfortable. He didn't mind. His mother cried sometimes, usually out of anger at something in the world she couldn't change. Dad just held her like this until her fury was spent.

After a long while, Jendyfi pulled away and wiped her eyes with her fist, smearing the green into streaks.

David said, needing to hear her voice grow steady again, "After that, you were on your own. How did you live? How long has it been?"

"A year." She produced a bit of cloth and blew her nose. "I brought some of the goats away with me for milk and turned the rest loose. I lived on milk and nuts and fruit, and rabbits and squirrels when I had to. I hate killing little animals. Snakes were easier, when I could find them." She saw his expression and smiled. "Snakes are good, fried."

"What happened to the goats?"

"The ogres found my cave. They ate them. I crawled into a crevice, far back. They couldn't reach in that far. I stayed still. They kept reaching, then started fighting over me, over who would get to reach in. When they were all hitting each other, I slipped out past them and ran. I thought I'd never make it, but they didn't even see me. I hid in a tree by the river.

"I lived on fish and roots for a while; then one of the wild pony mares lost her colt. They wander the woods all the time, but they're shy because of the ogres. I watched the poor mare, miserable with so much milk. I made a snare and caught her, and milked her into the leather bottle. She stayed with me until she didn't need milking anymore; then I drove her away."

"Why didn't you keep her?"

"Too risky. For both of us. I couldn't travel as fast as she could. And her scent drew the ogres too close to me."

"You miss her."

"I loved her. Everything . . ." She stopped and turned away. He felt sick for her—her parents, her sisters. He wanted to ask how many sisters, how old they had been; he wanted to know their names and if they had been like her, but he couldn't ask, it would hurt her too much. She said, almost as if she guessed his thoughts, "Do you have sisters and brothers?"

"No. Sometimes I wish I did. I have cousins, neat little kids. Some of my friends have brothers and sisters."

"Neat little kids?"

"You know—funny, smart."

Pain came into her eyes. Suddenly he didn't know what to say. They sat without talking, Jendyfi turned away, looking down into the woods.

After a while, their stillness grew easy again. She took an apple from her pack, cut it, and handed him half. "We'll go at dusk, I think. The ogres must have gone farther away than I thought." She saw his uncertainty.

"It will be all right; the ponies fill the ogres' minds. They can't think of two things at once. Except when—when the Degra tell them to do something. Then they . . . but the Degra won't bother with us."

"What are the Degra? Where are they?"

"The Undercity mostly. They're like men, but with sickly white skin, tall and thin and hunched, and their eyes are dark and empty, with dark circles around them; they have thin, long hands like claws. They haven't the souls of men, there is no caring in them, they love only evil. They keep thousands of slaves. They steal children for slaves from our farms and villages, and they breed slaves in the Undercity. They always have to replace them, because so many die. Sometimes they do things to the older slaves, experiment with them, change them into inhuman creatures to use in battle."

"Why did they attack your parents—*your* family?"

"They destroyed that whole part of the country. It was too prosperous, the goat ranches and farms too successful. We supplied a quarter of Meryn with food. The Degra don't like success—they want to rule all of Meryn, make all Meryn slave to them. A world of slaves—that has been their goal since they came here hundreds of years ago. Only the power of King Kastinoe stops them from taking over completely. But even Kastinoe is not all powerful."

When the forest began to dim and the wind stilled, they left the tree. Jendyfi had rigged a vine to pull the ladder up after they descended. They moved off quickly through the dark woods, listening for the ogres, ready to climb. Jendyfi said, "The moon will be up soon."

He longed for its light, but when the moon did come, its gleam through the branches turned the hills into a tangle of shadows that confused and tripped him. Jendyfi moved on easily.

Near midnight, when they were both yawning, they climbed into a tall tree, Jendyfi as comfortable in the branches as a squirrel. They ate two apples, some dried pears, and dried meat, David's mind filled with juicy hamburgers and fries and a shake. The woods stirred with flitting shapes and with the shrill cries of small creatures.

Jendyfi said, "Tell me about the game you play. Smacker?"

He laughed. "Soccer. You play it with a big leather ball. You can hit it with your head, your feet—anything but your hands."

"Yes, like pel-tranc. Who plays it?"

"People—anyone who wants to."

"Only humans? Not dwarfs or ogres—giants?"

"We don't have those in my world. Not real ones. Is soccer like the game you said?"

"Sort of. They play pel-traws at Caer Kastinoe. They play pel-tranc in the Undercity, only not with a ball. They play it with human skulls." She handed him a blanket, unrolled her own, and settled easily for sleep among the branches. He tried to tuck the blanket around him in the same way, and felt like a mummy.

The more he tried to sleep, the more awake he was, thinking of home. He thought Mom would have called Dad in England. They'd both be frantic, one on each side of the ocean. Or maybe Dad was on his way home to help search.

But if Dad left the dive, he might lose track of Balcher. And Balcher might get his hands on the lost medallion. Thinking about his father, David wished himself back home so hard it nearly made him sick. Why couldn't he make the medallion send him home!

He woke suddenly in bright moonlight, felt something sliding down his arm, saw a white hand clawing at him. A white creature big as a man hung above him in the tree, its mouth reaching for his throat, its pale wings rattling against the branches. He fought, twisting away. Too frightened to yell, he could only croak; but suddenly the medallion burned hot, and the creature jerked away screaming.

It crouched in the branches staring down at him, its eyes glassy and expressionless, then dropped toward him again; he swung out of its way and fell, grabbing a branch, then remembered the knife. Snatching it from his belt, he swung at the creature, slashing; at the same instant, he saw Jendyfi's sword flash, saw her blade plunge in. . . .

As the beast fell screaming, something black and huge dove past, filling the sky, and snatched it from the air.

The black monster folded its sweeping wings,

dropping down with its catch into the shadows beneath the tree. David listened to the wet, stomach-gripping sound as it crunched bone and flesh. Jendyfi's hand on his arm made him jump.

"It's all right, David. It's all right now."

"All right?"

"I'll explain in the morning. Go back to sleep."

"*Sleep?* You have to be kidding! What are those things?"

"The white one was a droowg, a creature of the Degra."

"And that black thing? It's as big as a barn roof."

"That's Haun. He'll protect us now. We're all right now, with Haun here." She moved away, yawning. The sound of crunching filled the night, then some strange rattles and bumps that he couldn't make out. Fear slid through his blood like a snake.

Jendyfi was soon breathing deeply. He lay crammed between the branches, tangled in the blanket. To ease his terror he filled his mind with the faces of his parents, made himself hear Dad's loud, reassuring voice and Mom's laugh, easy and careless, that meant everything was all right.

But it wasn't all right. Nothing was right. What was happening at home? What was happening to his father?

40

And was there some reason, connected to the Viking ship and the lost medallion, that he and the medallion had been jerked out of their own world?

chapter 5

Loud music woke David, brassy and wild, and he heard men singing and laughing. The morning sun blinded him. He stared down through the branches. Below him, six men were dancing around the tree, jiggling and hopping and shouting their song, and blowing on brass horns. They were warriors, heavily armed, dressed like the cast of a medieval adventure. Their armor looked well used, with dents in the metal and tears in the leather. One man's leathers were dyed in diamond shapes of red and blue and purple; he had colored scarves wound at his throat. Whirling, he played a concertina. They were singing about a prince and a maid, a smutty song that made David laugh.

Beyond the men burned a campfire with a pot

hanging over it. Nearby, blankets were thrown back. There was a wagon, big and square, like in pictures of gypsy wagons, its sides brightly painted. Four large horses grazed beside it, done up in jeweled harnesses. As David clung there, looking down, a wind nearly knocked him out of the tree: Black wings filled the sky as they had last night, and the monstrous black beast dropped past him directly at the dancing men, a creature longer than the four horses, with a black-scaled body like a giant lizard.

He landed nearly on top of the warriors and horses. The horses paid no attention, just looked at him sleepily and kept grazing.

He had a huge cat's head, like a black panther four times bigger than any panther David had ever imagined. His wings were sleek with black feathers, his silken, furred face long and intelligent. His cat eyes blazed very blue. At the other end of his long, scaled body, his waving panther's tail sported a glowing yellow stinger. His legs were a giant panther's legs, muscled and powerful. As he raised his muzzle to roar, his blue eyes caught David in a stare that made his heart miss.

"It's all right." Jendyfi put a steadying hand on his shoulder. "It's just Haun." At his frozen look, she smiled, amused at his fear. "He's a wyverlyn. There aren't many—Haun is famous all over Meryn. His full name is Haun son of Hual Huelo. I've never seen him this close. He's wonderful. He has a fierce reputation."

"I just bet he does. What—what does he eat?"

"Ogres and droowgs, of course. When he can get them."

"And in between?"

She laughed. "Fruit and berries. Nuts. I've heard he is fond of rabbit stew with dumplings." She laughed out loud at David. "He doesn't eat people, not human people. He won't eat you, David Shepherd." She looked down at the men, her brown eyes filled with admiration. The singing men were looking up and smiling and waving their brassy instruments.

"They are the Company of Haun," she said. "Meryn's finest warriors."

The wyverlyn reared suddenly, parted the branches with his huge black head, his cat eyes slitted, and thrust his black feline nose at David, sniffing him. His rasping breath stirred the leaves, warming him through. His long cat whiskers were pressed against his face by the limbs, his cat eyes now opened wide, each as big as David's hand, staring at him. David didn't dare move. Jendyfi straddled a branch and began to rub the beast's ears and stroke his cheek as she told David about the warriors.

"The smallest man, the one in the studded leather armor, is elven." The dark elven man, playing the brass horn, stomped back and forth in clumsy dance steps, his dark eyes flashing.

"The jester, with the painted leathers and scarves, is like us."

"Human?"

She nodded. "And their leader is Llellwyn, in the chain mail and scarlet cloak. Half human, half elven, he is." The blond leader played a flute, swirling his scarlet cloak as he spun. "It is Llellwyn who rides the wyverlyn," said Jendyfi. "The other three, playing the lutes, are brothers." She smiled. "Who knows what mixture they are." The three lute players looked much alike, big men with bland faces, their chain mail dull and dented.

Behind the men, on the brown hills, five animals grazed, slim as antelopes with straight, long horns. Their hides were scaled like armor, and they wore jeweled saddles and bridles.

"Gifetts," Jendyfi said. "They're called gifetts."

The jester began turning handsprings, then made his colored silk scarves fly into the air and vanish, then appear again, popping out of nowhere.

The wyverlyn licked Jendyfi's hand, his black tongue rough as a metal rasp. He gave her a penetrating look and left them, dropping to his four feet, where he curled up beneath the tree, folding his black wings. He began to lick his huge paws, and wash his face.

"Isn't he a love?" Jendyfi said. "In the villages, he lets the children ride him."

"He looks more like he'd eat them."

"Oh, but he's so gentle—except when he's killing droowgs and ogres. Come on." She slid past David down the tree toward the wyverlyn, casual and surefooted.

David followed, not wanting to be thought a coward—and caught his shoe in a wedge of branches so he nearly fell on top the wyverlyn. Jendyfi grabbed his arm, steadying him. The wyverlyn gave him an intent stare, then rested his panther's head on his heavy paws, yawning. His mountainous black body snaked away.

David stood very still before the wyverlyn as, again, he stretched out his huge feline head and nosed at him. He seemed particularly interested in David's soccer shoes, bending to smell them, his round black ears tickling his neck. But then suddenly he raised his head and stared at David with excited eyes, dropping one huge paw on his chest, pushing him backward against the tree.

David began to sweat. Laughter exploded from the warriors; they fell over themselves laughing, and Jendyfi was laughing with them. "If you could see yourself . . ." she shouted, holding her sides. "Your expression . . ."

He was about to say something to shut her up when the wyverlyn spoke.

"What are you cowering for, human boy? What do you think—that I will eat you?" His eyes blazed. "Eat *you*? A puny half-grown creature in funny shoes?" The wyverlyn roared with a thunderclap of laughter. "I eat *ogres*, boy! I eat droowgs! *Not boys in peculiar shoes!*"

The wyverlyn clapped his huge, soft paw around David's shoulder and pulled him against his scaly chest. He smelled like cinnamon, but his grip was like steel cables. He began to purr.

"I am Haun," purred the wyverlyn. "Son of Hual Huelo."

"Oh, yes," said Jendyfi. "Of course we know who you are—you are famous."

The wyverlyn rumbled with pleasure. "Yes. I am famous." He twitched his whiskers. "We are a company of the wyverlyn, warriors of King Kastinoe. And who are you, tender humans?"

"I am Jendyfi—I live in Cymru Forest. This is David Shepherd from—from I'm not sure where."

The wyverlyn squeezed David tighter, as if in acknowledgment of the introduction.

After a moment he said, "Our red-cloaked leader is Llellwyn, the only warrior fit to ride on my back."

This was not a modest wyverlyn.

"The only man fool enough to ride on your back," Llellwyn said. He looked David over, curious, but not unfriendly. Llellwyn's thin, sun-browned face was creased with laugh wrinkles; his eyes made David think of light-filled smoke. Beneath his red cloak David could see jeweled patterns worked into his chain mail. The leader touched fingers with Jendyfi, then with David, in a strangely formal greeting.

"Arean is our jester," Haun said, nosing at the warrior with the diamond-dyed leathers. "Our mage—and our thief. The lies flow from his tongue smooth as honey."

Dark-eyed Arean winked at David, a rogue's smile. He was tall and slim, well made. His many-colored suit hung easily. His eyes were so black, David couldn't see the pupils. He shifted his concertina so it belched out a sharp note, and put out his hand to them. But he watched David closely. "We're pleased to meet you, David of the funny shoes," said Arean, "and Jendyfi of Cymru Forest." He gave Jendyfi a long, charming smile.

The wyverlyn said, "The shortest one among us is our merry Morgo, impresario of the big brass horn."

Morgo grinned a silly, elfish grin and blew a blast on the shiny horn. He had a square face, a broad mouth, dark, laughing eyes.

"The most refined among us," said Haun, "are Difa, Glud, and Hew—excellent, bloodthirsty fighters."

Difa, Glud, and Hew shifted their lutes to

their left hands all at the same time, and made the same light, formal greeting with outstretched hands. They were twice the size of small, square Morgo. Though very big men, they were colorless and unremarkable compared to the yellow-haired leader with his swirling red cape, or the black-eyed, brightly robed Arean. Difa, Glud, and Hew's very ordinariness made David like them. Even Difa's voice was calm and low.

"Did you sleep soundly after the droowg tried to kill you, David-from-nowhere?"

"Oh, yes," David lied.

Jendyfi said, "We saw Haun and knew we were safe. But why did the droowg come? What would a droowg want with us?"

"Perhaps it was interested in young David," Glud suggested.

David frowned. "Why would it be?"

"I do not know," Glud said. "Unless the *Degra* be interested in you—perhaps because you are a stranger."

"But I— How could they even know about me?"

Morgo said, "They be knowing, young David. The Degra have their ways."

"The droowg last night," Llellwyn said, "surely it was sent by the Degra, possibly to observe you."

"But I— But why?"

49

"Only you can tell us that," Llellwyn said. "But the droowgs are the Degra's messengers and warriors. They move at the Degra's bidding. The droowgs are made by the Degra, a product of their dark powers."

"*Made?* A product? You mean it was—that the Degra created that thing? Like you would build something?"

"They form the droowgs from the bodies of dead slaves. They bring the slaves back from death with dark powers as they make changes in their bodies," Arean said. "It is a combining of dark spells and dark surgical experiments to change the body and to build the wings."

David felt sick with disgust. He could still see that wrinkled white face. That droowg, looking at him through slick eyes, had once been human. "But you . . ." He stared at the wyverlyn. "You ate that one last night. It was human." He was terribly, profoundly shocked.

Haun pulled David close, hugging him between big warm paws. "That creature was not a man anymore, David Shepherd. The man in him is free. Its soul has been released, freed to be born again. What I destroyed was only the dark terrible work of the Degra, better off destroyed, better off without a trace left in this world."

But how could he eat it? How could he eat such a thing?

Haun saw his distress and hugged harder, nearly smothering him; but warming and comforting, too, the way a big warm dog can comfort a frightened child. Then Haun pressed his panther's nose against David's chest; David could feel the medallion pushing hard against him. Haun's sudden shout nearly deafened him.

"Show us what you wear beneath your tunic, David Shepherd. What metal burns so warm against my nose?"

The medallion *was* warm. Was it going to take him home? He waited with rising excitement.

Nothing happened.

"Well?" rumbled Haun impatiently.

David touched the gold chain. What harm, to show the medallion? It would mean nothing to them. Anyway, Jendyfi trusted the Company. He drew out the heavy gold disc.

The Company stepped back from him.

Morgo's hands were raised, his square face startled.

Arean stood very still, his black eyes blazing. Difa, Glud, and Hew were arrested in mid movement.

Llellwyn's hand gripped his sword. His voice was hardly a whisper. "King Kastinoe's medallion."

Arean came close to David, looking. He did not try to touch the medallion. His scarves blew in David's face, his black eyes shone with challenge. "How can you have the king's medallion?" He grabbed David's shoulders suddenly in a bruising grip. "Who are you, boy? Where did you get this?"

Llellwyn pressed close, staring. "How? Tell us! How have you come by the king's medallion?"

David looked back at them, too amazed to speak.

Morgo saw David's confusion and reached to clap a warm hand on his shoulder. "The medallion be the king's greatest power—be the saving force of Meryn. How—how have you come by it? And when?"

Jendyfi was white, her hands clenched. David could see in her face that she would not have been so friendly, might not have helped him, had she known.

"But this is *not* Kastinoe's medallion!" Llellwyn said suddenly. "Look!" He reached, but still did not try to touch the gold. "Can you not see? Kastinoe's medallion has a chip at the left edge where a sword struck it, years gone in Kastinoe's grandfather's time." He looked around at the others. "This medallion is quite unblemished."

"So it be," muttered Morgo, studying the gold disc. "So it be."

Haun nosed at the medallion; then suddenly he leaped up, snapping open his wings, sniffing and lapping at the wind. "Ogres! I smell them! Droowgs!" Llellwyn jumped to his back and Haun swept straight up on powerful wings, bellowing, "Smite them—butcher them—roast and decimate them—massacre . . ." Banking high and fast, he disappeared in cloud beyond the hills. The gifetts had come running; the warriors leaped astride and pounded away. David and Jendyfi stood staring after them.

Along the top of the hills was a line of white. Boulders? No—not boulders. It broke apart, flapping up into the sky. As the droowgs sped at Haun and the warriors, the wyverlyn banked, meeting them head-on in a tangle of feathers and fur. But a dozen droowgs broke away and veered toward the wagon.

chapter 6

Jendyfi's sword flashed. David leaped to grab a droowg by the wing, driving his knive into its heart, shocking himself. He had never killed anything. Fear made them fight, ducking, slashing, until Haun drove the beasts off: The last droowgs flapped up into the wind like blown trash. Haun returned to the wagon licking blood from his whiskers.

The armored antelopes came galloping; the warriors slid down and stood looking at David.

"We have never been followed by droowgs," Llellwyn said. "Ogres, other goblins. Never droowgs."

Morgo slapped his gifett to send it trotting away. "The droowgs be wanting you, young David. They be wanting your medallion."

"How could they know of it?" David said.

"With the power of the Degra, they be knowing."

Llellwyn wiped blood from his sword. "Your medallion holds power, and the Degra can sense that power." The leader stopped polishing, giving David another hard look. "Where do you come from, David Shepherd? Who are you? How come you to own this medallion that is twin to our king's? Are *you* a king? A prince?"

"We don't have kings and princes in my country. I—I come from another world." David thought no one would believe him. But their looks did not change, except to grow more intent.

"Another world," mused Arean, his dark eyes burning.

"Whatever world you be coming from," Morgo said, "there be royalty in your family, or you would not be wearing the medallion."

"There was a king," David said, "hundreds of years ago." But he thought the warriors were too interested; they began to make him uneasy. He looked back at them defiantly.

"Tell them," Jendyfi said softly. "Tell them all you can. They mean only to help."

Morgo said, "Your father be descendant of this king?"

"Yes. But now . . ." How could he describe his world, his country, where there were no kings, but elected governments and corporations and committees? "My father teaches college. He's a professor of Welsh history and literature, and a track coach."

Morgo said, "Literature?"

"Yes, ancient stories. Like ballads, like what you were singing, only written down."

They nodded. Llellwyn said, "He does not sing his stories?"

"Sometimes. He teaches about the stories as one would teach—numbers, maybe. Well, yes." David laughed, hearing his father's booming voice in the shower. "Yes, he sings them, but in private. He doesn't carry a tune very well."

Arean grinned; they all laughed. "And you," Arean said, "do you carry a tune better?"

"Worse," David said.

"That be all right," said Morgo. "Why, the finest king in Meryn can't carry a tune, even in a barrel."

Llellwyn sheathed the sword he had cleaned. "And what is a track coach, David Shepherd?"

"Track is a running race. He trains the runners. He was a track star in school."

"I see," Llellwyn said. "And does your father look like you? The same blond hair and green eyes, and so strongly built?"

David nodded.

"And he was bearer of the medallion, before you?" said Llellwyn.

"Yes. The medallion was his father's, and his

father's, back more generations than I can count."

Llellwyn stood idly stroking Haun. "Do you know that there are three Medallions of the Black Hound? They were cast by a king of great power—and not in our world. Surely, David Shepherd, you come from the world of the medallions' beginnings."

Arean said, "Other travelers have come to Meryn before you. One such brought King Kastinoe's medallion to our world."

"When?" David said. "When did he come?"

"Nearly eleven hundred years ago," said Llellwyn. "He remained in Meryn, and became Meryn's first king. His heirs have ruled Meryn, and his medallion has protected Meryn, to this day."

The middle son, David thought, the son whose disappearance was never explained.

"The three medallions," Arean said, "cast half by skill, half by magic, were meant to protect against evil. But one was turned to evil."

"The medallion of the youngest son," said David. "But how do you know the story?"

"From the bearer of Meryn's medallion," said Arean. "From King Kastinoe. The history of the medallion has passed down to him as part of its legacy. Do you know of Finn Mac Cumhal?"

"I know of him. But what is the tale told in Meryn?"

Llellwyn sat down beside Haun, leaning

against the wyverlyn's shoulder, stroking him. "Finn Mac Cumhal was a strong king and a powerful mage. He made the three medallions to protect his three sons from a curse the Degra of that world laid on them."

"But there are no Degra in my world; I never heard of Degra until I came here."

"Are there evil, unnatural men in the history of your world?" said Llellwyn.

"Yes. They were called by many names, but not Degra."

Llellwyn nodded. "When they came into our world, they took the name Degra from a small, leechlike animal that sucks blood. In their mother world, as in ours, they used their powers for destruction. In their world, they rode the lanes at night with a band of wolves that would maim and kill."

Llellwyn's story was the same as the Celtic tale—how the wolves attacked the lady of Finn Mac Cumhal, and how Finn hunted them with his hounds led by Tuiren. How, when Tuiren and her pack killed the wolves, the evil masters vowed to destroy Mac Cumhal and his family.

"It was a few years after the ship sank and the youngest son was drowned," said Llellwyn, "that some of the Degra of that world found their way into this, to escape another great king who battled evil. They brought their dark ways here, seeking a world they could control.

"The king's middle son followed them, intending to destroy them. But in Meryn their power joined evil already here and became too great to destroy. That first bearer of the medallion was able only to contain the Degra within the underground city that they built. Though he brought together a force of warriors that has lasted to this day. He was ancestor to King Kastinoe; his heirs have been dedicated to destroying the Degra. But they have been able only to keep them contained.

"It is told that the oldest son left his home, too," Llellwyn said, "to cross the seas of his own world, to a new land." Llellwyn studied David.

"Yes," David said. "I am his heir. I wear the medallion of the oldest son. But it is very new to me—I don't know its ways. In my world, magic isn't a part of our life anymore."

How could he explain the powers that had replaced magic, the physical powers of electronics, chemistry, the instant communication brought about by satellites, the inventions made possible by space travel? These would be like magic to a world without them.

Llellwyn said, "Your medallion could not have brought you to Meryn by its one power alone, David Shepherd. Such power, to bring you from another world, must be linked to something else of power."

"Two medallions together be having such

power," said Morgo. "Your medallion, linked to the power of the king's medallion."

"Or," said Arean, "linked to the power of the Degra. Perhaps the Degra have learned to use the strength of your medallion to draw you here." Arean was looking at him intently, puzzled, but then the jester smiled and grew easy again.

Llellwyn clapped a strong hand on his shoulder. "Whoever brought you here, David Shepherd, whether the Degra or the king, you would be safest at the palace of Caer Kastinoe. There King Kastinoe will protect you. There your power *would* join with his."

"But I . . . How do you know I'm not evil, that I wasn't brought here by the Degra?"

The warriors laughed. Morgo said, "We not be training all our lives to fight evil without learning to recognize evil."

Glud said, "The Degra might indeed have brought you here, David. They might have intended to use you, but I do not think they can."

"We have looked on the face of the Degra and their pawns," said Hew. "You are not like them, David Shepherd."

Llellwyn said, "There is a warmth about you, young David, unlike the Degra and those who intend evil. You are," said Llellwyn, looking at him deeply, "you are very like King Kastinoe.

And I see the same honesty in your face. I see no malice there."

"But," said Difa, "Llellwyn speaks good sense. You would be safest at Caer Kastinoe."

"But I don't . . ."

Jendyfi said, "It's a long way over the mountains to Caer Kastinoe, and there are no woods to hide us. If the droowgs want David, they'll pick us off like ticks on a goat."

Llellwyn said, "You need not go alone; we will take you to the king—Caer Kastinoe is our destination."

Jendyfi brightened. But David thought this was too convenient, that they were too anxious. He didn't want to be told where to go or what to do; he felt maneuvered, used.

Llellwyn saw his distrust. "We are the knights of King Kastinoe, David Shepherd. All companies of wyverlyn are. All of us trained under Kastinoe, and trust him with our lives."

Morgo said, "Kastinoe bears the mate to your medallion. Do you think he be committed to evil? Only one medallion be committed to evil, David Shepherd."

The drowned medallion—the medallion Dad had gone to find. David knew he must trust these men, that he had little choice. He wanted to trust them. If he went with them, and if he *could* join his medallion with King Kastinoe's, maybe he could help his father somehow.

Jendyfi said, "I'll cook, to earn our way." She gave David a happy wink. "I have never been so far south as Caer Kastinoe." David looked at her brown-eyed, eager smile and felt easier.

The jester smiled back at her. "We're getting very tired of our own dull cooking. And, young David," Arean said, his black eyes teasing, "how will you work your way?"

"I can cook," David said. "And I'm a pretty good mechanic—well, with bikes and cars. Maybe wagons. I can use a bow," he said with inspiration. He had been on the archery team for three years.

"There are extra bows in the wagon," Llellwyn said, as if he expected everyone could shoot a bow.

"You can help care for the gifetts," Arean said. "They want much grooming and polishing and cleaning of feet, to be civil. Come, I will show you." Turning, Arean led him up the hill toward the scaled beasts.

David didn't see Arean grin, or the look of amusement on Morgo's face. He watched the gifetts grazing across the crest of the grassy hill, and climbing beside Arean, he felt a comfortable companionship. The jester moved loosely, easily.

He wondered what these fighting men would think of American soldiers—of an American army with its thousands of troops and tanks and electronic weapons—and planes? What would they think of jets? What would Haun think?

And what, David thought, would American pilots, flying into battle, think if they saw Haun flying toward them?

chapter 7

They knew they were being followed. It was their second morning traveling. Haun winged over them, watchful and nervous, his tail lashing against the wind, then flew low along the mountain looking into crevices and caves. They were headed south for Caer Kastinoe. David, Morgo, and Jendyfi walked beside the wagon, behind the mounted Company, through tall brown grass. David led Morgo's gifett, but with great care.

"Tomorrow," Morgo said, "we be crossing the bridge that spans the White Valley."

Jendyfi said, "Do we have to go that way?" She had a little twitch at the corner of her mouth that David had learned meant fear. He thought she did not like to show her fear.

"That pass be the only way between the

mountains," Morgo said. "It be five days' journey to go around, a dangerous, hard journey." He glanced up at the black wyverlyn winging over them. "With Haun, we not be having trouble at the White Valley, the Degra not be bothering us."

David didn't understand. "Is the White Valley a part of the Undercity? Is the Undercity so close?"

"We're a long way from the Undercity," Jendyfi said. "But not all the Degra are there. They come out into Meryn sometimes, trying to take over the smaller valleys."

Morgo nodded. "Meryn be divided by its mountain ranges—they be crossing one another like a grid. Fertile plains and cities lie between. The Degra be tunneling through the mountains, trying to start new cities in the narrowest, steepest valleys. We drive them back—when we first met you, we be coming from routing Degra camps. Always they be returning—return stubbornly to the White Valley."

David thought of the narrow Salinas Valley, where his aunt lived, or the Great Valley along the Appalachians. He and his parents had spent last summer there, while Dad did some research on how Celtic tales came to the New World. Both valleys were long and thin, hemmed by mountains. He guessed the valleys in his world weren't so divided by cross ranges, though—he knew enough geology to think that the formation of Meryn had been different from the formation of earth.

Jendyfi said, "Tomorrow—will you drive the Degra away tomorrow, from the White Valley?"

Arean turned in the saddle. "Not while you two travel with us."

"But they be fools to attack us there," Morgo said. "Haun be coming down on them—the droowgs not get away from Haun in that narrow space."

The gifett David led reared suddenly, balking, almost jerking the rope from his hand. He held tight, fighting it as the Company drew swords, staring around them.

They saw nothing, but the gifett would not go on until Morgo spoke to it. David led it with great respect; his shoulder still hurt where it had bitten him yesterday. When it had spit foul-smelling juice on him, the six warriors had laughed, teasing him.

He had only been grooming it, polishing its leathery scales; he had done nothing to make it mad.

"Gifetts be touchy," Morgo had said, finished laughing, scowling at Arean. "Arean not be telling you that. Some of us be having our jokes. Pay no attention to our fine jester!" Morgo had put his arm around David companionably, and given him some salve for the bite.

"You be earning the gifetts' respect slowly, young David. But they be good beasts, they be fierce in battle—against droowgs, against the Degra."

Even later, when Arean showed David how to groom the beasts so as not to anger them, the jester was still smiling at his joke. Changeable as quicksilver was Arean, easy and comfortable one minute, wild with some teasing the next. David had watched him play pranks on all the members of the Company—all but Haun. Arean didn't tease Haun.

The warriors, except Llellwyn, had grown up together as orphan wards of young King Kastinoe. Morgo said, "Arean be the prankster among us even when we be small—played tricks on all the palace.

"Arean's father be the court magician, my own father a court minstrel. They have some wild times together. We apprenticed to them as young boys, learned juggling and magic tricks and songs, until—until they be killed in battle."

David felt Morgo's pain, felt suddenly closer to the elven man.

Jendyfi gave Morgo a little hug. They had both lost their families, and at about the same age. All killed by the Degra. David watched how the sun glanced across Jendyfi's brown hair, how light her walk was, and easy.

After a while Morgo continued, quietly, "Difa,

Glud, and Hew be the sons of a military captain. He be tortured to death by the Degra. All our mothers be members of the king's militia. All killed. All our families killed, in the War of Midnight, when the Degra attacked Caer Kastinoe.

"After that, defenses be increased, outlying patrols be given regular quarters. Now Caer Kastinoe be circled by guard stations."

As they drew nearer the White Valley, David grew strangely uneasy.

"It be evil you feel," said Morgo. "The breath of evil seeping out from the White Valley."

David thought they were all aware of that breath of evil. They moved on, tense and alert. He said, "A teacher told me once there are many kinds of evil. That evil was complicated, hard to understand. My father said that was rubbish."

Morgo laughed. "Your father be a wise man, David Shepherd. Some men be making evil into a fascinating subject. Not so!" Morgo's brown eyes flashed. "All evil be amounting to the same thing." The elven man looked deeply at David. "What be the evils of your world?"

David thought about it. Some things were hard to explain. What could he say about Mr. Rolf except that he frightened everyone? He couldn't say *why* he was evil, but David knew he was. And getting his bike broken—compared to some things, he guessed that wasn't so terrible. He told Morgo about shipwreckers of the last century luring cargo ships to smash on the rocks, leaving the crew to drown in heavy seas while they stripped the ship of its gold. He told about the medieval practice of cutting off an enemy's hand or foot or plucking out an eye, punishable by only a fine, and often done in the name of religion. He told about the clubbing of baby seals in the Arctic. The look in Morgo's eyes was deep with disgust.

"The evil be all the same," Morgo repeated. "The wreckers, the vengeful men you speak of, and the Degra. Even in small evils, David, the *intent* of evil be the same."

David guessed the cold intent *was* the same. "But the Degra—what exactly are the Degra? Are they human?"

"They be shaped like men, but they be of more ancient, dark-minded races that lived in your world before the coming of men. They be thin, white-skinned creatures, bloodless, with eyes like dead-black holes—empty eyes circled by darkness."

Jendyfi said, "They love human suffering. Last year, they burned all the crops in the north so the farmers must starve or come crawling to them as slaves."

"Some be escaping to Caer Kastinoe," Morgo said.

"But many did starve," Jendyfi said. "They wouldn't give in."

69

"Evil be a gluttony for power," Morgo said. "A lust to control every living thing—control by enslaving, by hurting, by depriving." His face was not merry now. "It be my people the Degra have enslaved, more than any others on Meryn."

Jendyfi said, "When the Degra first came to Meryn, they used their dark powers to lure elven folk down into the mines. They had powers to confuse them, make them obedient. They made them carve out the Undercity. That's how it was built, by millions of elven slaves digging, shoring up. Millions died in cave-ins. My father said . . ." Her jaw went tight. "My father said the Degra turned millions of people into beasts duller than any animal.

"And—and the Degra took all the elven babies born in the Undercity—took them from their mothers. They still do that, take the babies as soon as they are weaned and put them into prisons to train them. When the children can hold a pick, they are made to work the mines."

"Those children be knowing nothing else," Morgo said. "Never see the daylight, work the mines in darkness until they die."

"They don't rebel?" David asked.

"The Degra," Jendyfi said, "keep their minds too dulled to think about rebellion. The slaves live hundreds together, they don't know enough even to wash themselves, they get a new bit of clothing when the old rots and falls off. You can't imagine what they are fed. They breed and have babies that are taken away from them to start the horrible business over again. They live worse than any farm animal."

Morgo said, "They be having no learning, no experiences to understand other ways. They be having no idea there is another way to live. But the Degra be living in fine houses in the Undercity, in grand caves with every elegant thing, be having gold furniture, fine food all bought with the gold and gems the slaves mine."

"But the house servants," David said, "don't they see all that?"

"The minds of the house servants be destroyed by the Degra's powerful magic. They have no thoughts, no desires. But there be another class of elven. There be elven who are not dulled but who love the evil of the Degra. They come aboveground to do the Degra's work secretly, to try to convert others to the Degra, and to spy on the king's armies."

Before they stopped for the noon meal, Difa and Hew killed and skinned three rabbits. Sitting around the fire as Jendyfi and David fried rabbit, the men kept their weapons near. And as they sang, David turned, amazed, to listen. He knew these songs—these were Celtic ballads, the ancient songs his father collected. Dad had hundreds of tapes; he had done his master's thesis in Wales, before David was born, and had taped songs and folk tales. Their house was often full of lively Welsh music. Now, listening to the familiar songs, David was gripped by homesickness.

He supposed King Kastinoe's ancestor had brought the Celtic music to Meryn, just as it was carried from Wales to the American colonies. Hearing it in this alien world should comfort him, but it didn't; it only made him lonely. He was struck suddenly with rage at whoever had brought him here.

He saw Jendyfi watching him and grinned at her, trying to put aside his anger, letting Morgo's song fill him; the elven man's voice was true and rich as he sang of the fideal, a monster born of marsh grasses.

> *"A young prince sought the fideal,*
> *And wrapped himself in grasses.*
> *He caught the fideal, caught it,*
> *In a net of woven grasses.*
> *He drowned the fideal, drowned it,*
> *In the waters of Cymru Loch."*

Then Arean sang of the hobyah:

> *"Down Cymru coast it wandered,*
> *But it feared the hounds there.*
> *Hobyah run and run from them . . ."*

Arean's black eyes sparkled.

"Down Feff's Wood, a hound catch hobyah,
  Drag hobyah 'round the countryside,
  One day, two days, three days, four . . ."

He was joined by the clatter of lutes and the horn.

"Five days—six days—seven days—eight . . ."

David could almost hear Dad singing along with the tapes. Jendyfi took his hands, swaying her shoulders with the music, singing so lustily he couldn't help but join her, as badly off-key as his father.

She said later, as they were washing the tin plates beside the wagon, "The songs made you think of home—they were songs you know, weren't they? From—the country of the medallions?"

"Yes, Wales."

"You miss your home."

"I guess."

She looked at him, waiting. He didn't want to talk about home. He almost said that she had never talked about her home, after that first time, but he didn't. And then, because she looked disappointed, he told her about spending the summer with his aunt in the Salinas Valley, picking beans and strawberries and swimming in the Salinas River. He had to explain even the smallest things. Jendyfi had never tasted a straw-

73

berry, didn't know about bees and honey; Meryn's plants were pollinated by minute winged lizards. He discovered quickly that there was little he could tell about his world if he left out machines. Strangely, he didn't want to tell her about machines or planes or cars; he didn't understand why. Except it would get so complicated. And it would sound to her like a new kind of magic. And she might feel very deprived afterward, and unhappy. He didn't even try to describe ice cream, because she would ask where they got the ice.

When they moved on, Haun swept close along the mountain, listening as a cat listens for mice inside a wall. "Ogres," he growled more than once. "Following close, in their tunnels." And then at nightfall, when they made camp, Haun left them for a long time, returning with five bloody ogres' scalps to drop at Llellwyn's feet.

David slept little that night, lying beside the wagon, staring up at the unfamiliar patterns of stars. The immensity of the universe, or perhaps of an alternate universe, was almost more than he could handle. And he felt as if something nearby, dark and chill, was reaching out to draw him in, and wondered how much the medallion *could* protect him.

And wondered who had brought him here, and why.

Then, half asleep, he felt his mind fill with

his father's voice: *This power . . . holds for its bearer a solemn commitment.* And David thought, I must honor the medallion's power just as my father would. I don't know why I'm here, but I must face whatever comes—I must do what Dad would do.

He watched Haun drop down out of the sky, looming over him, felt the wyverlyn's warmth as Haun settled carefully between him and Llellwyn, his wings spread to cover them. All night Haun had been diving and settling and lifting again, anxious and muttering. David relaxed under his warm black wing, protected and secure, and soon slept.

But in sleep he was restless; faraway voices seemed to whisper to him from centuries before he was born, frightening and challenging him.

chapter 8

The party, walking single file, was descending a narrow trail between cliffs when suddenly the mountain ended: Empty space yawned before them. David caught his breath, staring down into a mile-deep white chasm.

Far below, the pale valley floor was piled with white boulders as round as the skulls of giants. Slaves moved among them in long lines, carrying rocks out of caves. Many were children. On the other side of the chasm a ridge of white mountains rose. The swinging bridge crossing to it seemed to David thin as a thread.

He tried to push back his fear, but the wind hit him hard, like hands shaking him, as if the world were tilting beneath him; he knew he could not cross that empty space. Shaken, he thought something didn't want him to cross, wanted him to fall.

The wagon moved out ahead of them onto the span, its wheels filling the bridge so fully they were nearly over the edge. Difa drove it casually; Morgo followed, glancing back for David.

"I can't," David said.

"Go on," Arean said behind him. "Haun is above us. If anyone fell, Haun would snatch them up. It's all right, David. Go on."

He couldn't.

"Go on," Arean said crossly. "It's the Degra making you afraid. The longer you wait, the worse it will be. Defy them! Get on with it!"

Haun descended beside him, hovering, tilting, Llellwyn looking across wind and space at him from between Haun's wings. "Go on, David. Now."

He trusted Llellwyn, knew he had to do this. Haun hung on the wind beside him safe as a wall. Sheltered by Haun, weak with fear, he stepped out onto the narrow span.

He tried to walk steadily, but the drop-off on the side away from Haun pulled at him. He moved ahead slowly. When he glanced down at the cliff, he was startled to see it writhing: The white stone walls were alive with clinging droowgs, their flat faces turned up to watch him, so intent he thought they were waiting for him to fall. Below them, in the valley, three thin, hunched men watched too. David swayed, frozen.

"Go on!" Arean shouted. David felt a wave of terror when Arean's strong hands clutched his shoulders; but Arean was only supporting him. He was dizzy, confused, and then he stopped still as a vision filled his mind: The bridge seemed to have vanished. He was in a room, surrounded by slaves that reached and cried out to him.

Within the stone room Degra men worked over a table on which lay slaves' bodies. They were grafting bony wings onto the already deformed bodies, chanting heavy spells as they joined bone and muscle and skin. David felt sick, his head rang with the slaves' cries of pain as they were slowly transformed into droowgs; soon their bodies were no longer human, everything human was gone. Stiffly the newly made droowgs rose from the table reaching for David, whispering, *Come close—come close to us. . . . Be one of us.*

But then as he watched, phantom shapes thin as smoke drifted over the mutated bodies, bright, lifting up out of them, swirling out, rising. He could almost see human form, yet these beings were more than human, more beautiful, shimmering. The medallion burned him; he felt a power touching it and touching him, a power as if from far beyond the chasm. He watched the souls of the mutilated slaves lift on the wind, reflecting light, rising swiftly until they became far, glancing lights leaping across the sky; he watched until they were gone.

Arean's strong hands held him. He remembered where he was, saw the bridge beneath his feet, the yawning chasm. Hot rage filled him, and he shouted down at the Degra, his voice rattling across the chasm, "You didn't destroy them! You didn't destroy their souls! You can't!"

The Degra men drew back.

"You only destroyed their bodies!" His blood was pounding.

The Degra men turned, disappeared into a cave. The droowgs clung to the sheer cliff, wailing. David felt Arean and Morgo supporting him between them, leading him on. He pulled away and went on by himself, unafraid.

That night beside the campfire Llellwyn said, "The Degra do not find it easy to bring visions. It surely cost them something to create that vision in the valley."

Arean nodded. "Can their powers have increased suddenly? How else could they have made such a sharp picture?"

"And the other vision," Llellwyn said, looking at David. "The vision of the escaping souls. The Degra would not bring that." All the Company was looking at David, waiting so intently he felt his face flush.

"I didn't bring the vision. I don't—I've never tried such a thing. Something else brought that—something powerful."

Jendyfi said, "Was it—the same power that brought you here?" She reached to touch his hand, searched his face.

Llellwyn shook his head. "Surely it was Kastinoe who brought David here. You know, David Shepherd, that two medallions together can foster other powers?"

David frowned. "The tales of my world say, *Powers not known—powers forgotten . . .*"

"Perhaps forgotten in your world," Llellwyn said. "Kastinoe believes that the powers possible between two medallions can extend the magic of vision. Can reach out beyond vision, and move the subject of that vision to another place. He says those powers can go inward as well— that they can touch the inner strengths of someone worthy and needing, give strength to one failing."

Llellwyn was very still, then said softly, "If Kastinoe did not bring you, David Shepherd, perhaps you *were* brought by a greater power—by the force that gave magic to the medallions. By the power that made us all."

chapter 9

The fifth night they approached the small village of Belmath, climbing the steep ridges in blackness, fighting a cold wind. Faint moonglow showed, high above them, a tangle of stone cottages crowded between boulders. They struggled steeply up to it, looking forward to hot apple beer and a good fire, a hot supper and hot baths and real beds; and a good rest and feed for the tired mounts.

The wind whipping across the mountain scoured Belmath's empty streets. Only a few lights showed behind shutters. David had gotten used to the dense darkness of Meryn nights, traveling in the empty valleys and mountains. He had nearly forgotten streetlights. But now, coming into a village, he felt that the darkness seemed strange again. There should be lights near houses. Not until the horses and gifetts clattered stumbling along the cobbles toward the town square did lamps begin to flare behind windows.

And then soon doors and shutters banged open, heads were thrust out, and greetings shouted. Now the townsfolk came streaming out around them laughing and shouting, some still in nightshirts.

"Haun—it's Haun!"

"The Company and Haun! Oh, bless them!"

"Haun and our warriors!"

"It's all right now!"

"Haun—Llellwyn—the Company has come at last!"

Haun stretched out across the cobbles, his long body curving to the walls of houses and shops. Night-clad children scrambled onto his back or stroked his silky face or pulled his whiskers, talking to him all at once like a flock of chattering sparrows.

A dozen young women surrounded Arean, laughing with the jester and flirting with him. Shouting, he lifted one, then another, to whirl her around and give her a kiss, his bright, diamond-patterned clothes catching the light, his eyes flashing.

Two lanterns burned before the inn. David and Jendyfi could see through the windows the round, aproned innkeeper stirring up the fire and laying on logs.

They stabled the horses and gifetts and, though tired and hungry, the Company sang half a dozen rollicking songs. Arean did magic tricks and tumbled while the girls clapped and laughed. But soon they headed for the inn, the townsfolk surging along with them.

The inn was old and small, with just four bedrooms to let, and its tavern so cramped that four tables crowded it. But the fire was roaring, and the elven proprietor brought crocks of hot apple beer, then hot soup and platters of cold mutton and fresh bread. Townsfolk crowded the room. Most of them were happy and laughing, but there were dark stares, too. Morgo, looking away from two angry elven men, said softly to David, "I not be calling all the elven my people. The elven be split as sharp as a melon halved." He ladled his soup, scowling. "We be in Caer Kastinoe not soon enough for me."

The elven innkeeper was saying, ". . . it was two days ago that Caer Kastinoe was attacked by the Degra."

The warriors stopped eating and stared.

"How heavily attacked?" Llellwyn said. "What was the damage? What of the king? Tell us, man! What has happened to the king?"

"Kastinoe is safe. His armies hold the city,"

said the innkeeper. "All is well now. The Degra did not attack the city proper, but burned many of the city's farms. Crops and orchards were destroyed, goats and sheep slaughtered—perhaps a fourth of the city's food supply. Word has it that suddenly the Degra have set out to conquer *all* of Meryn. There have even been Degra soldiers here in Belmath. Nine of our men were killed before we drove them out. Word is, the Degra want to chain us all in the mines—take all our towns and farms for themselves."

"They don't have that kind of power!" Llellwyn said. "They can't conquer all Meryn!"

The innkeeper dropped his voice. Talk resumed around them politely, though some ears strained to hear.

"Something strange is happening, Llellwyn. There is a change in the Undercity, an alarming increase of power. Strange things are happening all around us in the mountains. Destruction, terror in the villages; men and women and children fleeing, sometimes wounded, always sick with fear.

"It is said that the king's troops pace in their eagerness to attack. But that, strangely, Kastinoe waits. Word is that he has sent captains to the two kings of the North to rally their forces to join him, but—I don't know. It is most strange that he has not moved more forcefully."

Soon after supper Jendyfi disappeared to bathe.

Buckets of steaming water waited in the bedrooms, set over coal fires, but David followed Morgo to an icy waterfall behind the inn, unwilling to seem a sissy. There they bathed in the freezing snow melt, Morgo splashing and gurgling happily.

"Be the best bath in Meryn," the elven warrior bellowed, laughing at David. David nearly froze until he dove right in; then soon he was tingling warm. Morgo finished first, but waited for him, passing him the soft lump of lye soap, watching the shadows. David wondered what Morgo would think of indoor plumbing and hot showers. He smiled, thinking of his mother. She would endure camping, ticks and chiggers, eating cold beans from a can, hiking in wet boots. But she detested doing without a hot tub or shower.

Mom would love the inn, he thought, would love supper before the fire, with the inn's dark coarse bread and rich soup.

It was not until later, back in their crowded room, that David discovered he had forgotten his knife when he had dressed.

He waited until the Company slept. He didn't want Arean's teasing because he'd lost his knife; the jester would make the most of that. He knew it was foolish to go out alone, but he could almost see the knife fallen among the boulders; it would take only a minute. He went down the stairs in darkness and through the empty tavern.

As he searched for the fallen knife, he thought a shadow moved among the shadows of the cliff. He stood looking, but nothing more stirred. He felt for the knife and found it wedged between rocks just where he had thought it was. But then as he turned away toward the inn, he froze: A man stood before the cliff. David tried to judge whether to run or to fight.

The man was thin and tall. He wore a battered hat, and his thin shoulders were shrugged down inside a shapeless jacket. David realized that the rock cliff shone through his body, that he wasn't real, and started toward the vision angrily; but suddenly other figures moved out of the darkness, surrounding David. They were real; one gripped his arm with a hand cold as ice. Degra—five white-faced Degra men, thin and gangling, their dark-rimmed eyes expressionless. The hand holding David chilled his whole arm.

When the others reached for him, he shouted "*Bran!*" and the hound exploded into the night, immense, lunging and snarling at the Degra; they crowded away, pressing against the cliff. But the man in the vision had turned, his hat was brushed off, and David went cold with shock, remembering a news photo, staring at the man's completely bald head crossed by a thick scar. *Balcher*—heir to the third medallion. David's fear made him falter so badly that Bran vanished.

He could not bring Bran back: Terror more powerful than normal fear, gripping like giant hands, had emptied him of strength. The Degra pushed close to him. "Remove the medallion. Put it on the stone."

Shocked, David didn't move.

"Put it on the stone."

He tried to back away, and could not, a power of cold terror held him.

"Lay the medallion on the stone."

He felt weak, unable to resist.

"Put the medallion on the stone."

Woodenly he reached to his throat. The chain was choking him. He lifted it, but the medallion burned his hands, he dropped it again as Bran flickered like a shadow, then vanished. Balcher's power was strong. David fought the man, pushing back the terrible weight of fear; and his father's words exploded in his mind: *He must be stopped. . . . Balcher must be stopped.* At last he pulled himself from the bald man's hold; as the vision of Balcher vanished, David attacked the Degra with his knife, cutting one, shouting for Bran. Bran burst among the Degra, now, snapping and bellowing. The Degra ran, disappeared into a cleft in the mountain.

David knelt, hugging Bran, feeling the big

hound's shagginess and strength, and breathing in his wild scent; and thinking about Balcher.

Surely Balcher had the third medallion, to be able to show himself in a vision. But where was he? Still at home—in Wales perhaps? Near the dive—near Dad?

When Bran, not needed, vanished, David was shaken by an aftershock of fear.

He got back to the inn fast, was nearly to the room he shared with the Company when the door flew open and Morgo surged out, armed, coming to look for him. David collapsed against him.

All the Company was awake, dressing to come after him.

"I—forgot my knife—by the waterfall."

No one said anything.

"There were men there—Degra. Five Degra. But there was a man who wasn't Degra. I saw him in vision, I could see the cliff through him and—and I know him."

Still they waited, their attention fully on him.

"He is a man of my world. He is of the blood of Finn Mac Cumhal, a descendant of the third son. He, and the Degra, tried to make me give them the medallion. But I think . . ."

He saw Jendyfi slip in from her own chamber, to stand against the little side door.

"I think he has the third medallion. His name is Balcher." Why hadn't he told them about

Balcher before? But he hadn't dreamed before that Balcher would have anything to do with Meryn. His concern, when he had thought about Balcher, had all been for his father.

He told them about the dive, about the Viking ship, about how interested his world was in the ancient weapons and tools. He told them how Dad had found out who Balcher was.

Llellwyn said, "How old was the ship?"

"About eleven hundred years. The Vikings used to sail from one land to another, killing, plundering gold and jewels. They stole from the Celts, from the country of Finn Mac Cumhal. There were Celtic pieces on the ship, swords and jewels and chests. And Finn Mac Cumhal's sword was there—embossed with the black hound. That was why my father thought the third medallion might be there.

"But—was this a vision from my world? Could Balcher be that powerful? Or," David said, feeling cold, "or—is Balcher *here*?"

The Company was quiet. Then Llellwyn said softly, "If Balcher appeared to you in vision, he could, indeed, be here in Meryn."

"I *hope* he's here—I hope he's not in my world—I hope my dad's all right."

"If Balcher is here," said Llellwyn, "and wears the third medallion, you and all of Meryn are in danger."

"I didn't mean—I meant . . ."

"We know what you meant," said Arean. "But Llellwyn speaks the truth. If the third medallion is again in evil hands, and is in Meryn, that danger is close to us, very real."

"And I," said David slowly, looking from one to another, "I'm sort of in the middle, aren't I? Like the soccer ball being kicked between the teams."

Jendyfi looked shocked. Arean's face twisted into a wry smile. Llellwyn and the three brothers didn't change expression, or speak.

"Not fair," said Morgo. "Not a fair or kind thing to say."

"I'm sorry," David said. "I'm being rude. Maybe—maybe I'm a little scared."

Morgo put his arm around David. "You be not alone, David Shepherd. You be not alone in this. We not be abandoning you."

"If Kastinoe brought you here," said Llellwyn, "then we are committed to helping you. If you came to Meryn by power of the king, then you are our sacred charge."

chapter 10

Sliding down loose shale, the gifetts descended the mountain, swinging around boulders, moving light and fast. David rode behind Morgo, Jendyfi behind Arean. They had left the slower wagon and horses in Belmath and were heading for Caer Kastinoe. Haun's shadow swerved along the mountain's rocky face as the wyverlyn searched for anything that followed. Halfway down the mountain they entered into mist, low and thick. As David clung to Morgo, Morgo described the island city, then told about growing up in the palace.

"We be living in the soldiers' wing," Morgo said, swaying easily with the descending gifett. "When very young, we be pages, then later trained as knights. We all be growing up at Caer Kastinoe, all the Company except Llellwyn.

Llellwyn be living in the high, misty mountains on his father's sheep and goat farm. Llellwyn be a dreamer; but one day Llellwyn be seeing his first wyverlyn soaring in the sky above the high peaks. Then all the dreams come together. Nothing else would do—he would be a Knight of the Wyverlyn."

"And he chose Haun?"

Morgo laughed and slapped his thigh, startling their gifett so it lunged. "No one choose a wyverlyn. Haun be choosing Llellwyn. In the Ritual of Acceptance, the wyverlyns be choosing. That day," said Morgo, shaking his head. "That be a day to remember.

"In the city square, it was. Twenty youths battled each other in turn, watched by three young wyverlyns. Haun be the oldest, so he be having first choice. Young Llellwyn, he be winning all the battles—he be Haun's choice, all right."

"There!" Jendyfi cried. "Caer Kastinoe!"

The blowing mist had tattered into scarves. Beneath it, down the mountain, ran a wide green valley carved into squares of orchards and vegetable farms. The riders were still so high that David thought their view was like looking out the window of a plane. He wondered again what the Company would think of airplanes, these medieval folk with their own winged steeds.

Just beneath them, at the base of the mountain, the farms were burned black in a long scar. David could see blackened fruit trees, burned houses and barns, and their burned smell came sharp on the wind. Beyond the burn, a lake sprawled across the valley, and in its center rose the island, crusted with rooftops and crooked streets. He could see the pale spires of the palace, rising tall.

A thin causeway crossed the lake from the south, another to the north, the only ways across the huge natural moat that protected the royal city. But, David thought, droowgs could come at it from the sky. Caer Kastinoe looked like medieval cities in pictures, walled and protected; he knew it would fascinate Dad.

He was stiff from riding the swaying gifett; the metal studs in Morgo's armor pressed hard into his chest as Morgo leaned back for their descent to the causeway. David looked up enviously at Llellwyn and Haun, winging free in the cold, sharp wind. The wyverlyn shone like ebony against the clouds. Mom loved anything that flew, birds, airplanes. What would she think of Haun? David grinned, imagining her amazement.

He missed home again suddenly, painfully. As the gifetts swung out onto the causeway, his mind was filled with his mother's face, with Mom home alone trying to go to work every day, worried about him and about Dad.

His mother had to work really hard this time of year. An accountant with her own business, she did nothing but work in the spring, putting in twelve-hour days and more on her clients' income taxes. She was always distracted then, getting home after dark, going to work before it was light. Dad and David did the cooking during the pretax months. Only, this spring Mom and David had done it together, heavy on TV dinners.

And now, Mom was alone. The world of home, of getting meals in the bright kitchen, seemed remote and unreal. He brought it back deliberately, the winter months when he and Mom had breakfast together, his mother's clatter as she made pancakes, her voice asking what he wanted in his lunch, the smell of syrup, then peanut butter, filling the kitchen, kids shouting for him outside. Huddled against Morgo, afraid again as they approached Caer Kastinoe—afraid suddenly of meeting the king—he held the sense of his mother close.

The lake on both sides of the causeway was a heavy, dull gray. The gifetts swung along in single file. At the city gate Arean roused a sleeping guard, and they passed through into the crowded streets, Haun roaring in the sky above them. At once people burst out of shop doors, shouting and laughing.

"The Company! Llellwyn!"

"Haun!"

"Come down, Haun!"

"Music—give us song!"

"Haun—come down and let us ride!" shouted the children; and folk crowded around them so thick that the gifetts could hardly move. But beyond the laughing faces were unsmiling elven men leaning in doorways, watching.

Arean cleared the way by balancing on the back of his trotting gifett, juggling three knives; the crowd drew back to give him space, and the Company came behind. On the broad square before the palace, Haun stretched out full length across the grass, mobbed at once by screaming children hugging his thick legs, reaching for his ears. The warriors made song as they were expected to do; to go directly to the palace would cause questions. But David felt edgy, wanting to be away from the crowd.

Soon he would be face to face with Kastinoe. Was it King Kastinoe who had lifted him out of his own world, into Meryn's private war?

At last they moved on into the palace, leaving their mounts for the king's soldiers to tend. David went slowly, increasingly uneasy, reluctant to meet the king.

After the bright, warm courtyard, the central hall was cool and shadowed. The stone walls rose three stories to a balcony, then to a high domed ceiling painted with flying wyverlyns.

But it was the portraits of Meryn's kings, hanging lower on the walls, that made David stare.

Here were all the Kings of Meryn, generations of kings crowned in gold, robed in furs and silks. Each one wore the Medallion of the Black Hound, passed down the generations, the gold disc repeated in each painting. Yet it was not the medallion that held David but the kings themselves: their faces, their eyes, their shocking familiarity.

The Kings of Meryn were broad-shouldered, square men, square faced and light haired, so much like family pictures of David's own ancestors, so much like his own father, that he stood lost in them until Jendyfi took his hand.

"Come on, David! What's the matter? Oh—yes," she said, grinning at him. "Yes, you are like them. The same green eyes and light hair, the same features." She touched his cheek, winked at him. "Handsome as the Kings of Meryn," she said, laughing with pleasure, then pulled him away to stand with the Company.

A delegation had gathered, crowding the hall, yet hardly seeming to fill its cavernous, stone-girded space. And David saw that here, too, were men watching with the same sour intensity he'd seen in the square. Llellwyn said softly, "We will not speak of your medallion yet. There is a new steward, a man I do not know." He pulled his cape around him, watching the steward approach: a tall, dry-faced man.

The steward led them to a chamber lined with books and more paintings of kings, where they could talk undisturbed. He stood before the hearth, facing them. David slipped to one side, out of the way of the Company. The paintings hung behind him. The steward stared at him so intently that he stepped back again, wanting to lose himself in the shadows.

The steward said, "Do your knights include children now, Llellwyn?"

"David and Jendyfi are apprentices of song and of magic tricks. They are to be trusted. You may speak freely before them."

"So be it." The steward looked hard at the Company. "You seek conference with King Kastinoe."

"Of course," said Llellwyn.

The steward shook his head. "That is not possible, it is too late." His face was closed and pale. Morgo started to speak, then went silent. The Company waited, tense.

The steward continued, his voice slow and tired. "The king lies ill. We cannot wake him. Kastinoe is aware of nothing."

David saw disbelief on the faces of the Company, then suspicion, then pain.

Morgo said, "Be not possible! Not Kastinoe!"

"What kind of illness?" Llellwyn said sharply. "What has happened to him?"

"We think—perhaps poison," said the steward, "though the physician cannot be sure, does not know what kind of poison it would be. There were tasters. Everything the king ate was tasted, but—the truth is, no one knows. No one knows what to do for him."

Llellwyn said, "We must see him. But first— that is not all your news."

The steward nodded. "The Degra are growing bold. Before he took ill, Kastinoe was preparing to ride north, to rally the Northern kings. He had already sent messengers, but he meant to go there himself, to bring the Northern armies here, then march on the Undercity. Kastinoe meant, this time, to destroy the Degra."

"Destroy them!" Morgo said softly.

"Before they destroy Meryn," the steward said. "There is, in the Undercity, a sudden and alarming power. A power that, if it is not stopped, I fear will soon enslave all of Meryn.

"And there is restlessness among Kastinoe's armies, a troubling dissent. For the first time, in my lifetime," said the steward, "we have had desertions."

"His men love him," said Llellwyn. "They would not . . ."

"But they have. You know yourself, Llellwyn, that for the four years since the accident the king has been—not as aggressive, perhaps."

Llellwyn nodded. "We have prayed he would mend, be himself again."

David glanced at Jendyfi. The Company hadn't mentioned an accident. Jendyfi shook her head as if it was something they didn't like to talk about.

The steward's eyes showed a deep, steady grief. "There has been no change in the king these last weeks. And now, as the power of the Degra has increased—now a man has appeared in the Undercity, a man known by no one."

David went cold. No one moved. The warriors' eyes were hard.

"He holds the power to destroy all of Meryn. The king knew—before he took ill, he knew."

"What power?" said Llellwyn softly.

"This man . . ." said the steward, his voice low, "this man—wears a Medallion of the Black Hound."

There was a long silence. Then:

"Describe him," Llellwyn said.

"A thin man and bald, with a scar across his scalp. He wears the medallion, twin to the king's medallion. It has been seen by our spies in the Undercity.

"Its power shakes Meryn," said the steward. "Its force threatens the power of Kastinoe—perhaps this power alone holds him unconscious. Perhaps, despite his inability to move or speak,

the two medallions are somehow locked in con-
flict.

"Nothing seems able to break it. Nothing.

"Come," he said. "Come to his chambers."
He glanced at David and Jendyfi as if he thought
they should not be included.

"They must come with us," said Llellwyn. "It
is urgent that they come."

The steward's eyes widened.

"They are our charges," Llellwyn said. "We
cannot leave them unattended in the palace. Too
many faces, now, that do not look sympathetic
to—children."

The steward led them through the corridor
and up a wide flight, to a short corridor ending
in double doors. He pulled the doors open and
stood aside, speaking with Llellwyn, then left
them. Morgo took David's hand, drew him into
the big, shadowed room toward the huge, can-
opied bed. David could see in its shadows the
heavy bulk of the king's body beneath the cover,
a powerful man lying asleep, his face turned
away, his golden beard spread across the pillow.

David moved around the bed until he could
see the king's face.

The resemblance to his father was strong.
King Kastinoe was an even bigger man, heavier
boned, powerfully muscled. The line of his jaw
was wide, square, made heavier by his thick
golden beard. His lashes were golden, his brows

thick and wild, with some of the hairs curling. His skin, even in this unnatural sleep, was ruddy and tan. Kastinoe's forehead was square, the bones of his face prominent, as if they had grown stronger than the bones of ordinary men and were bursting to grow even more, to form this warrior into a giant. Suddenly, crazily, David wanted to hug him, wanted to wake him and talk to him, tell him everything that had happened. He reached out toward the king, caught in a pain of longing. . . .

He looked up suddenly to see Jendyfi and the Company watching him, and realized he was clutching Kastinoe's shoulder, gripping the king's hard shoulder, his knuckles white.

Jendyfi's eyes met his, trying to understand what he was feeling. He eased his hand from the king's shoulder, backed away. They stood quietly looking at the king. Around them, the big, shadowed room was ornate with tapestries and carved furniture and tall, draped windows; but the bright, commanding, powerful heart of that room was the sleeping king, like a golden statue hidden beneath covers.

chapter 11

Llellwyn was the first to speak. He jerked his cape off, dropped it on a chair, shook the king trying to wake him; then turned away irritably and began to pace. "Kastinoe has never been ill. If this is poison—we must learn quickly who could be responsible—how many changes in the palace—how many trusted servants replaced." He turned to look at Kastinoe again, frowning. "And yet—his color is high, his breathing even. . . ." Llellwyn spun, facing David.

"David Shepherd, if it is the power of Balcher's medallion that holds Kastinoe, can you help him? Can you wake him?"

David touched the gold chain around the king's throat, then turned back the cover so the king's medallion shone up at him. He touched the gold disc, touched the nick at its edge, looked closely at the hound. She was more finely made than Bran, as a bitch would be. "Tuiren," he whispered, then looked up uncertainly at Llellwyn. He didn't know what to do, or even how to begin.

"You must use the power of vision," Llellwyn said. "And then you must reach beyond vision. I think you must draw forth his deepest thoughts, find something whole and untouched deep inside, if you would wake him.

"You *must* destroy the force that holds him. If he remains asleep, the Degra will attack. They thrive on weakness."

Morgo glanced toward the door. "We be remaining with you, young David. A guard be always with you."

Llellwyn said, "If Kastinoe brought you here— if he brought you across worlds with the power of his medallion joined with yours, then you must learn to join and use that force as strongly."

If there is time, David thought. If I have time to figure out how, before the Degra attack.

The Company ordered cots for all of them set up in the king's chambers, and a screen placed across a far corner to give Jendyfi privacy. Soon the warriors began to move about the palace taking care of duties, gathering information, asking questions. Always one or two remained with David and the king.

All afternoon David sat beside the huge bed, willing Kastinoe awake, trying to draw from the two medallions a power of life. But each time he thought he had woven some strength between the medallions, some power to touch the king, he felt that strength drain away. As evening dimmed the tall windows, he began to think he could not wake Kastinoe.

"Rest," Jendyfi said. "You were tired from our journey. You'll be stronger tomorrow. If we could get him to eat—some broth, maybe . . ."

Llellwyn ordered broth from the kitchen, Morgo held the king's head up, and Jendyfi tried slowly dripping a little broth into Kastinoe's mouth.

It did no good; the king wouldn't swallow. When their suppers came, Jendyfi waved her fried venison before the king, hoping the good smell would stir him. It didn't. "I guess the homely things like broth and venison won't help. I guess it really will take magic. I guess you will have to wake him, David Shepherd."

David sat down on the bed, trying again to imagine the king awake, to picture what the king would see as he woke: the Company still seated around the table; and David's medallion shining above him, to join its power with his own. He tried hard to put that picture into the mind of the king.

Nothing happened. After a while, he whispered for Bran: Maybe the hound could wake Kastinoe, the wild scent of him, the feel of his shaggy warmth pressing insistently against the king.

Bran did not come. Surely the power that held the king kept him away. Stubbornly, David settled down to try alone.

He stayed with the king very late, at last falling asleep on the king's pillow. Arean woke him.

"Come, that's enough for tonight. Perhaps, before you can succeed, you must build your own inner forces."

"I'm using everything I have to use."

"I think," said Arean, "that the secret lies in giving Kastinoe's own strength back to him." Arean's black eyes looked hard at David; he was not the lighthearted, teasing jester now, but grimly serious. "A man's strength is in the things of life he most values. I think you must learn what Kastinoe values—must know him better, must learn his innermost concerns, the things important to his life. Only then, perhaps, can you touch him deeply enough."

"Then tell me about him—everything about him."

"Come sit down. It's a long time since supper. Morgo has brought some cold lamb and bread, a pitcher of milk."

David collapsed on a couch next to Jendyfi. He'd never thought how hard an effort of the mind could be—harder than all-day soccer or football practice. He dug into the food, starved. "Tell me about the accident the steward spoke of. No one told me about that."

"It is painful for us," Arean said. "We do not talk of it easily. The queen and their only son were killed four years ago, in an avalanche.

"Their party was traveling to the northern forest to join the king to hunt deer—the queen, some palace women, many children. Half the mountain slid down. A terrible death, a terrible loss. The king loved her very much, loved their little child very much—had such dreams for him. And the queen—she was an amazing and beautiful woman, red haired and slim as a reed. A fine, capable woman."

"Everyone told tales of her beauty," Jendyfi said, "and of her hunting skills. I never saw her, but everyone said she was the loveliest woman in Meryn. My sisters . . ." She stopped, looked at David. This was the first time she had spoken of her dead family since that day in the forest. "My—sisters used to dress up and pretend they were the queen. Every traveler who came by our farm told tales of her. My little sisters longed to be like her."

"She was the finest horsewoman," Morgo said. "She trained many of the army mounts. And she loved their little boy so dearly. Young Prince Kastin be only a tiny boy when he died—

he be just three. After the avalanche, searchers be finding the queen crushed beside her mount under boulders. Her twelve ladies be found, but not all the children. There be nineteen children dressed in traveling leathers like the young prince. Only four bodies be found. No one be knowing which of the little crushed bodies be the prince.

"Kastinoe's soldiers be searching among the rubble, tearing the mountain apart, moving boulders. All the land be searched for children maybe dazed, wandering away.

"Nothing more be found," Morgo said. "Nothing."

"What caused the landslide?" said David.

"The Degra made it," said Llellwyn. "It was not the first time they killed that way. The soldiers found evidence of many tunnels and narrow fissures dug in a webbed pattern all through the face of the cliff."

David went to stand beside Kastinoe's bed, looking down at him.

In sleep, did the king grieve for his family? Was that grief a part of what held him so silent and still? And was Kastinoe aware of his own forced sleep? Did he, somewhere inside himself, fight with cold panic against that dark emptiness?

chapter 12

"Those be grand days, when we be boys and Kastinoe be training us." They sat at breakfast in the king's chambers. "Twenty, thirty children," Morgo said, "he be raising us like his own. He be hardly more than a boy himself."

"Kastinoe was seventeen," Glud said, "when King Kendennel was killed by the Degra." He glanced at his brothers. "Our father died by his side."

"At that time," Arean said, "there were many more ogres in the land. The Degra sent them thundering into Caer Kastinoe suddenly one night. Our troops killed many, but at great cost." The jester's eyes were dark with remembering. "I was very small. Most of the children were hidden in cellars to escape the slaughter. When the battle was over and the ogres driven out, the survivors came for us. My parents were dead . . ."

"All our parents were dead," said Difa. "King Kendennel was dead."

"The orphans were brought to live in the palace," said Arean. "A few days later, young Kastinoe was crowned king. Soon he began to train the children. I think that in his grieving over the death of the king, he determined never to let Meryn be beaten again."

"Kastinoe be teaching us the sword," Morgo said, "oh, he be a hard foe. And in battle—that Kastinoe be wild in battle."

"Oh, yes," Jendyfi said, "everyone says he's as fierce as a wild bull—the fiercest king in Meryn's history."

"Kastinoe trained us hard as horsemen," Difa said. "What demands he made of that band of little boys!"

"Sometimes," Arean said, "I went to bed so tired I cried, certain I could never do all he expected."

"But you did," Jendyfi said. "All of you did. You are the finest warriors in Meryn."

Morgo said, "We be responding to that challenge. Kastinoe be expecting much of us, and that be a good way to teach children."

"Yes, my father . . ." Jendyfi began, then looked down, her face filled with pain.

"Your father?" said Llellwyn gently.

"He—expected a lot of us when we cared for the goat herds and the farm, and when we hunted. He was demanding. He wanted to make us strong."

"You be very strong," said Morgo, putting his arm around her, drawing her close. "He be proud of you."

As the warriors told of Kastinoe's battles against the Degra, and of the atrocities committed by the Degra, David understood sharply their terror of living as slaves in the perpetual darkness of the Undercity mines. His father had once described slavery as a destruction of all possible choice—choice about where you could go, what work you could do, where you lived, what you ate or *if* you ate. A slave had no choice about whether he was beaten or starved, or forced into crippling hard labor.

The greatest barrier to enslavement had been the king's medallion, stopping the Degra from bold attacks. Now, without the king's conscious direction, that medallion was no barrier.

I must wake him!

Now, with Balcher here, only the two medallions together can save Meryn. He sat down on the bed beside the king, his hand on Kastinoe's shoulder, trying to bring strength to the big, powerful man. Trying not to laugh at himself because he had the nerve to think he could help this fierce king.

There was no one else to do it. He must find a way to give his own strength, the medallion's strength, to Kastinoe.

David tried for hours that bled into days. Jendyfi stayed close, turning away quietly when he grew cross with her in his disappointment. Always she would turn back to smile at him, supporting him. And each day David came to know Kastinoe better through the Company's stories. The warriors were always near when he rested, when he took a meal, spinning new tales of Kastinoe. David grew to know each warrior better, as well, for their lives were intricately woven with Kastinoe's. He knew Llellwyn's dreams of the sky as the little boy had stood alone among his craggy mountains. He felt Morgo's pain as a small child, that his elven people were enslaved. He learned to know Meryn itself, the mountains and the life-giving rivers, as Llellwyn told him of the battle of the waters that Kastinoe waged constantly against the Degra.

"In the North," said Llellwyn, "in Kastinoe's realm and in the two kingdoms beyond it, the crops are watered by trenches from the rivers. If the rivers go dry, the crops and pastures die and the villages are soon without food.

"For many years the Degra, with slave power and with their dark magic, have carved out underground passages to divert our rivers and turn the upper lands dry.

"The king has battled them, has worked in the trenches beside his men, to return the rivers to their channels. But always," Llellwyn said, "the Degra return to do their mischief again."

Llellwyn looked hard at David. "Kastinoe has sweated and suffered for this world. He has put everything of himself into its well-being, into keeping Meryn safe—into keeping the Degra from destroying it and enslaving us all. He has lived his whole life for Meryn and its people.

"The Degra have taunted him, thwarted him. They killed the queen and their child. And now—*this curse of sleep must not destroy him!*"

"I'm trying," David said, bowing his head beside Kastinoe, forcing all his strength into a sense of power and well-being. He tried to bring alive feelings and pictures that would have meaning for the king: the vision of a slim red-haired woman turned away—he wished he knew her face—then the palace as he had seen it from the square; the faces of the Company; Haun winging over them . . .

He imagined a powerful destruction of the Degra, filled himself with a sense of victory, praying that feeling would touch Kastinoe.

Soon he became so attuned to the king, he began to sense Kastinoe's pulse increase and, counting the heartbeats, saw that he was right. He tried again to bring the hound into Kastinoe's chamber, but he could not; trying, he felt darkness pressing hard against him.

Jendyfi and the warriors brought David food, and Jendyfi tended the king, washing his face, combing his hair. She offered every kind of delicacy from the palace kitchen to tempt Kastinoe, letting the good smells drift under his nose; but nothing roused him. Then one morning David was stubbornly trying to bring a new vision for Kastinoe, of open sky and of wyverlyns soaring, when he saw the king's eyes move beneath closed lids.

For a moment he watched, not speaking, holding the vision as powerfully as he could. The king's lids moved again, his hand moved. David turned, barely whispering. "Llellwyn! Arean!"

The Company gathered. Jendyfi touched the king's forehead.

Kastinoe's breathing came faster, his hand moved on the cover. His mouth twitched.

"He's waking!" Jendyfi whispered. "Oh, he's waking!"

But suddenly the king's pulse went slow and uneven, his breathing shallow, and as David fought for him, something began to draw David into that same darkness. The figures around him grew hazy, the room darker. He saw Jendyfi reach out but could hardly feel her hand on his arm, could hardly keep his eyes open.

"David! No!"

He jerked awake. The room swam, sleep sucked at him. He pulled himself back.

For two days David fought the unnatural sleep, jerking himself back from darkness, fighting weakly for himself and for Kastinoe. And now a dark vision filled his mind, nearly destroying him: He could see his father trapped beneath the sea, fighting the sea, and he heard his father crying out to him.

Part of him knew the vision was a lie, but yet he was terrified. He tried to tell the others what he saw.

"A false vision," Llellwyn said angrily. "A lie, to weaken you. They are giving you a lie—as they tried to destroy you in the White Valley."

Jendyfi's look was desolate, as if she wasn't certain he could fight this.

Stubbornly and slowly he began to push back the fear, to convince himself the vision was false; but he was so tired, weak from the heaviness that filled him. He fought, his breath choking him, his skin clammy, until at last a new strength began to fill him. Now, again he roused—like running another mile when he thought he couldn't, like swimming another ten laps after he thought he was done for. At last he put the dark view of undersea aside, convincing himself it wasn't happening, hadn't happened.

He let different visions come, unfamiliar

scenes that, he realized suddenly, must come from Kastinoe—from behind that sleeping mask. Sharp but fleeting they flashed across his thoughts like charges of electricity striking between the two medallions. Each picture was vivid: a woman gowned in silk, red haired and beautiful, and David could see her face clearly. Then the same woman holding a baby. He felt Kastinoe's rage at the Degra, and Kastinoe's fear for Meryn.

He stayed beside Kastinoe's bed all night, now touching the sharp, living spirit of the sleeping king, trying with all his power to wake him.

And just at dawn, as the first gray light smeared the tall windows, Kastinoe woke. Suddenly his eyes were open, the king was looking at David, green eyed and alert.

At David's startled summons, the warriors were there, tense with excitement.

The king looked at them, frowning and puzzled. His voice was hoarse. "How long have I slept? When did you come, Llellwyn—Arean?"

They all tried to speak at once. Kastinoe reached to Morgo, and the elven warrior clasped the king's big hand in both of his.

"Something dark," Kastinoe whispered, "dark places—strange dreams, years of dreams . . . *How long have I slept?*"

"Several weeks," said Llellwyn.

"The Degra . . ." The king tried to rise, flinging back the covers, steadying himself against Morgo.

"There has been no attack," Llellwyn said. "Meryn remains free."

The king looked hard at them all. But then he looked at David, stared at David's medallion, reached to touch it. "You have come, David Shepherd. It was you pulling me back from the dark."

"You know my name."

"I had to know your name to call you from your world."

"You *did* call me!"

The king took David's hand; his hand was huge, warm, as he pulled David down to sit on the edge of the bed.

"Do you know of the third medallion, David Shepherd? The medallion turned to evil? Do you know that it is here, in Meryn?"

David nodded.

"Before I slept," said the king, "I saw it in vision. I saw it lifted from its hiding place deep beneath waters—from a sunken ship. There was a ship waiting on the sea above, not a ship from my world.

"I saw in vision a bald man moving about that ship at night, alone. I saw him take the medallion, drop the chain around his neck. I watched him leave the ship stealthily in a small boat.

"Soon afterward," said the king, "Meryn faced powerful new attacks by the Degra." He looked up at the warriors. "Llellwyn, gather the armies. Prepare at once to ride on the Undercity."

Llellwyn stared at him, did not move.

"What are you waiting for?"

"I think secrecy would be well—that perhaps there are traitors in the palace."

"Then call my most trusted captains. We will tend to traitors."

Jendyfi said, "You mustn't get up yet—you must gain back your strength."

"And who are you, young lady, to tell a king his business?"

"My name is Jendyfi. My father was the finest goat keeper in north Meryn. I have watched how hard David fought to wake you. I want to see you stay awake and get strong."

"I am strong now! What do you mean, your father *was*? Do you speak of the goatherder Jendyvran?"

"He was my father. He was killed by ogres, my whole family was."

"Oh—not Jendyvran. How long ago?"

"A year."

"And I did not hear of it." The king pulled her into the shelter of his bearlike hug. "Jendyvran was a fine man."

"Please," Jendyfi said, leaning into the king's comforting hug, "you must rest." Her look was so stern and caring that the king leaned back against the pillows, laughing at her.

David said, "What happened after the attacks began?"

The king frowned. "There were reports from our spies in the Undercity that a foreign man had come there. They swore he wore a Medallion of the Black Hound. Soon I knew his name.

"It was then I reached out in vision to search for the medallion of Bran, sure that only its power could help me. I found you in my vision, David Shepherd. You were standing in a room with wide windows and a white-blossomed tree outside. A dark-haired woman was with you, and a man . . ." The king smiled. "A man as familiar as if he was my own brother.

"He was placing the medallion around your neck. I saw your look of amazement, and his stern face. It was a powerful moment for you; I think that very power helped me to touch you in vision.

"I knew I must bring you to Meryn, that only with the power of both medallions could Balcher's threat be broken. I saw your name as if blazoned across the medallion, and with all the strength and magic I had, with all the power of Tuiren, I called you from your world—you and Bran.

"I had no idea whether I succeeded. The sickness took me—Balcher knew, Balcher tried to stop me." The king nodded. "But Balcher was too late.

"The power you brought to wake me was not easy, David Shepherd."

"Did you know I was trying?"

"At first I knew nothing but panic, trapped speechless and unmoving within my own body, held by a cold, debilitating fear, an emptiness I could not break through. It seemed forever that I fought. And then, when I was ready to give up, I became aware of you, David, reaching out, offering me strength. And then memories began to touch me."

The king paused, looking hard at David. "What is it, David Shepherd? Something is troubling you."

"I saw my father in vision. I know it was a lie, I know Balcher made me see him, but— he was beneath the sea, drowning, struggling. . . . My father—went to that ship, hoping to find the third medallion before Balcher did."

"You fear for him." The king sat up straighter against the pillows. "Perhaps together we can see—bring another vision of your world."

They tried, silent and still, their minds forced toward David's world and the drowned ship. But after a long time, when no vision came, David could see how much this effort drained the king. "Enough," David said at last, bitterly disappointed. "Later we can try."

Kastinoe frowned, moved again to get out of bed, then lay back weak. He scowled at Jendyfi. "Maybe our goat girl is right, maybe I need a few hours to mend—but I can't give in to weakness long."

"You be resting awhile," Morgo said. "Be regaining strength wisely, if we be riding on the Undercity."

Kastinoe's look livened, then flamed up at his warriors. "It's not rest I need, it's food! I'm nearly starved to death! Don't any of you know when your king's hungry! I want steak! I want chops and bread and pie! What are you waiting for!"

chapter 13

It was midmorning. The king had finished a huge breakfast and was pacing his chambers, giving orders to the warriors. David and Jendyfi were on their way with Morgo to the kitchens for a bite to eat. Morgo said, "Be eating nothing but food from a big pot cooking for the whole palace. Be telling no one the king has waked— the chef be thinking those steaks were for us."

The kitchens were three high-ceilinged rooms connected by arches, crowded with tables and storage bins, and pungent with the hot breath of roasting meat and bread and pies. A hard-faced woman blocked their way, a lean, muscled creature with wiry hair tied in a coarse knot atop her head. She looked them over with distaste.

"You are not allowed in here."

"Not be allowed? We be coming here every

day!" Morgo made for the stove, where a pot of stew simmered. The woman stepped in front of him.

"I am in charge of the kitchen today. No one is allowed."

"We only came in for a bite to eat," Jendyfi said softly. "It's a long time yet to supper."

Morgo found bowls, began to dish up stew.

"If you want food," the woman said, "I will serve it."

"We dish our own," said Morgo, blocking her reach.

"Do you have spoons?" Jendyfi said with studied softness.

The woman looked at Jendyfi as if she'd like to drop *her* in the stewpot; but when Morgo brought the stew to the table, she produced spoons. No one asked for bread. They ate quickly and left, still hungry.

"Her name is Prudd," Morgo said later, having talked with the kitchen help. "She be in the kitchen only a few weeks—assistant to head chef in a few weeks! The steward hired her at his recommendation. Before that, she not be known by the palace staff."

Prudd was not assistant for long. By nightfall nine members of the palace staff had been locked in the cells for sedition, Prudd and the head chef among them. Because of her manners and strange ways, some of the loyal staff thought that Prudd had once lived in the Undercity. The king's guards questioned her, but she told them nothing. All day there were conferences, orders given, the king's angry voice thundering behind his closed doors.

"Kastinoe be his old self!" Morgo said. "Getting things done now!"

Kastinoe paced his chambers shouting orders, but he still tired easily. They would ride on the Undercity as soon as the full army had gathered from outlying villages; but Jendyfi said, "It's too soon. He's not strong enough."

"He'll be strong enough," David said. "He has to be—he wouldn't go, otherwise." The strength of the attack would depend, in large part, on the power of the medallions. Kastinoe meant to find Balcher, to take the third medallion from him, and to completely destroy the Undercity.

Yet despite his confident talk, David was stiff with fear, though he would not have turned away. Something of him belonged to Meryn now, and to Kastinoe and the Company.

Evil was no different here than in his own world, slavery and despair no different. His mother and father had taught him to face challenge, to fight for right. Because of them, the blood of Finn Mac Cumhal spoke to him, strengthened him.

He did not let himself think that he might not get out of this; that he might not see his world again and his family.

The palace staff moved quickly to prepare supplies. Messengers had been sent, and troops began to arrive from outlying farms and villages to join the regular army. David stood at the chamber window with the king, watching the newly arrived soldiers making camp in the square, pitching tents, tending horses. Kastinoe said, "Can you handle a horse, David Shepherd?"

"I don't know. I never did, but—"

"If you never did, you can't. Arean will see that by tonight you can manage a war steed. Make sure he finds you some boots that fit properly. You cannot ride, or go into battle, in those strange shoes."

David thought of a plunging war horse, saw himself casually astride. It couldn't be so hard: a bit of balance, a few pointers from Arean.

Learning to manage a war horse was the hardest work he'd ever done. Arean started by making him saddle and unsaddle his horse again and again, until he did it fast and exactly right. Then he learned to mount the same way, mounting over and over until, when Arean slapped his horse to make it leap away, David swung aboard easily. Only then did Arean let him ride.

First Arean made him ride with no hands on the reins as the jester led the wheeling, cantering gelding. Arean's own horse was collected and watchful. At last David gained his balance and learned to stay with the quick, sometimes plunging animal. Thus he learned to guide and direct his horse with his weight and the pressure of his knees.

After the noonday meal, when Arean allowed him to take the reins, David's touch was gentle and for direction only, not to keep himself in the saddle. Now he could feel what his mount intended, and they soon became a team. As the afternoon waned, David and Arean played tag on the galloping horses, so David could learn even better balance and control. Then he practiced with a sword, against a straw-stuffed leather dummy. As evening drew down, they rode out across the hills with the Company and Jendyfi; she looked easy and at home on a big white mare.

Late that night, standing wakeful at the chamber windows looking out to the torchlit square, David heard Kastinoe stir. The king joined him, his broad-shouldered silhouette so like Dad's that again David felt fear for his father and missed him sharply. Kastinoe's face, in the faint light, was drawn and tired.

"Was Arean a good teacher, David Shepherd? Did you have a hard day?"

"It was hard." David smiled. "Arean is—the kind of teacher they tell me you were."

The king chuckled. "I was rough on them. I expect your leg muscles are sore."

"I didn't know I could be so sore. And I didn't know there was so much to learn."

"That is often the way. Something looks so easy, you think you can just naturally do it." The king hugged David companionably. "You have learned in one day what it should take weeks to master. But," said Kastinoe, "you had little choice." He stood looking down at the square, at the small leather tents and the dark forms of sleeping soldiers. David thought of the bright pop-up tents sold in the stores at home.

"Those men and women are more than half our auxiliary troops," Kastinoe said. "The rest of the outpost guards I leave to defend the city." He nodded toward some buildings across the square. "The regular troops are housed there." The king grew silent. Then: "You are afraid. That is natural. You would be a fool and a poor soldier if you had no fear. It is how you handle your fear that matters."

The reality of what they would face had begun to gnaw at David. This was no game, and no nightmare from which he could wake. They would ride at dawn to face a threat so powerful, so inhuman, that perhaps none of them would escape.

Perhaps Meryn itself, as a free world, would cease.

"The power will come to you," Kastinoe said, "as it will to all of us. One can do much more than one thinks."

"Are you saying we can't lose?"

"No. I could not promise that. Though I do not mean to lose. I am saying that our own inner powers will strengthen us, and thus the power of the medallions will rise stronger. Beyond that, we can only pray."

But David did not like the tired look in Kastinoe's eyes. He thought that battling Balcher's dark sleep had weakened Kastinoe more than the king would admit. He returned to bed, but slept restlessly and didn't want to wake when Arean shook him.

The room was still dark and cold. He rose, dressed, and ate the porridge, bread, and cold meat that had been brought to them. Jendyfi was quiet. She ate ravenously, as if she didn't expect another meal for a long time.

Their armies moved out in the predawn dark, David yawning and half asleep in the saddle. They crossed the southern causeway in darkness, and soon could smell the burned land, invisible around them. By the time the sky began to lighten, they were rising between the last green farms up into the mountains, the lines of armed troops silent; soon they were climbing steeply.

Two days' ride brought them across the rough,

forested mountains to the last ridge. There they dismounted, hidden from the plain below by a stand of fir trees. The well-disciplined soldiers made little noise as they fed and tended their mounts. The king quieted his horse and sat looking.

Far across the plain rose some low hills, like an island on the flat land. "The Undercity," Llellwyn said. "Those three caves mark tunnels leading down beneath the earth."

"Be an hour's ride," Morgo said. The sky was beginning to darken toward night. Nothing moved on the hills or the plain. David could see nothing alive.

"The sentries be hidden," said Morgo. "They be watching these mountains, all right."

They camped well back from the ridge among the trees, made no fires. David fed his horse from the rations he carried, and hunched down beside Jendyfi to eat his dried meat and bread. The sky was black; a sweep of stars hung low over the plain. Once alien to David, now they were familiar. The moon rose behind cloud, barely lighting the distant hills. David didn't want to talk, just wanted to be near Jendyfi. He needed to get through this, to give all of himself to the medallion at the right time.

Well before dawn they were winding down the mountain through the cold dark and out onto the plain, moving as silently as horses and gifetts could. Overhead Haun drifted, visible against the stars, then lost in cloud.

Halfway across the plain Degra troops exploded out of the dark; spears rang against metal, found flesh; the horses reared and screamed as ogres wrenched the king's men from their saddles. Haun dove on the attackers as Bran and Tuiren appeared, leaping, tearing, their roars drowning the shouts of Degra warriors. Above them, Haun cut down flying droowgs; Kastinoe's troops fought as one, until the Degra army panicked and began to retreat.

But suddenly, stopping the retreat, a wall of giants burst out of the night—not ogres but creatures that seemed tall as mountains, lumbering black against the stars, snatching up Kastinoe's soldiers, toppling horses like puppies. The hounds grew thin as smoke, faltered, vanished. As David strained to bring them back, he saw the king slumped over his horse, blood gushing from his side. Before David could reach him, Arean had grabbed Kastinoe, holding him in the saddle.

They were driven back—David could not bring the hounds; the king was losing blood fast. In the first dawn light, David saw the blow across Kastinoe's forehead, already swelling. A vision of Balcher's face, twisted with laughter, filled David's mind as a new wave of Degra troops charged, a Degra sword slashing inches from David's throat. Fighting, he saw Hew caught up in a giant's hairy arms, saw a giant shove Glud's horse down. Kastinoe was slumped against Arean, but David shouted, "Bring the hound! Help me!" The whole side of Kastinoe's body was dark with blood. *He is dying,* David thought. "Bring the hound!" he yelled at Kastinoe, sick with fear for him.

Kastinoe started and rallied; both hounds appeared, then disappeared again. David forced his horse close to Kastinoe. The king's look was not of a fighting monarch now, but confused. Balcher was doing this, Balcher and the Degra, and—maybe—David's own fear.

Their army fell back, loose horses stumbling over dead bodies. The third medallion was destroying them. Balcher and the Degra destroying them—and David could not battle him, his medallion seemed to have no effect. And he thought with despair, *Balcher cannot feel fear. I can't touch him.* As a new wave of giants bore down on them, suddenly Kastinoe rallied, staring at David. "Get away! Get away from them! Make one medallion safe!"

"No!"

"You must!" Kastinoe's eyes blazed in his swollen face. "Do as I command!" Kastinoe's horse reared suddenly, and a giant jerked the king from the saddle. He fought, shouting, "Morgo—get David away!" as he was lifted

against the giant's chest. The monster turned—
David lost sight of the king. Desperately, David
lunged his horse at the giant's legs, sword swinging, but Morgo grabbed his reins, jerking them
burning through his hands, pulling David's
horse around so hard it nearly fell.

"No!" David yelled; he saw Haun dive, saw a
giant swing, grabbing Haun, shackling his
wings. Morgo hit David's horse and they were
pounding away from the battle.

"Let me go! I won't leave the king!"

Their horses plunged into the face of their own
oncoming troops, snaking headfirst between
them.

Morgo pulled him on until they were so far
away the battle was only dust. Lost—they had
lost. Only at the edge of the wooded mountains
did Morgo pull the horses up.

"Why?" David shouted. "Why! We deserted
him!"

"You must keep your power safe until we fight
again."

"Fight again! He'll be dead. It's too late!"

"You would have died there, both medallions
be lost."

"But the king! You have abandoned the king!"

Morgo led the horses toward the trees. The
pain on his face was terrible. "The others will
protect him as best they can. I did as he ordered."

David could feel the elven man's wretchedness, but could feel no sympathy. Behind them the dust was settling. One rider pursued them, crouched low.

David watched Jendyfi come, not knowing how to face her. He had not helped the king, he had not been strong enough.

chapter 14

They dismounted, walking their heaving horses among the trees to cool them. Across the plain they could see long lines of their own, captive soldiers being forced toward the Undercity gates. David thought of their men lying dead or wounded on the plain, and was sick. A few small bands were still fighting valiantly but uselessly against the waves of Undercity troops. Jendyfi was pale, quiet. Morgo, too, was silent, all three of them caught in the agony of despair, and in the horror of the king's capture. Filled with defeat, David tried, still, to help Kastinoe.

Jendyfi said, "How *can* Balcher be so strong? How can he overpower the strength of *two* medallions?"

"Something my father told me about Balcher.

He said Balcher is a psychopath, that he doesn't feel fear like normal men. And the medallions' strongest weapon is fear."

"But what about the hounds?"

"Their power to create fear—like a physical sickness—that's their greatest strength."

"But with two medallions against Balcher . . ."

"If he doesn't feel fear, Jendyfi, how much could they touch him? And we— The king was more weakened by Balcher than we knew."

"And now, David? What now?"

"I don't know." He handed the reins to Jendyfi, and moved away from her and the horses, by himself.

Standing alone, looking off toward the Undercity, he tried again to bring a shield around Kastinoe. It seemed futile. He tried to call Bran and could not, so how could he help Kastinoe? Balcher was too strong. Yet he tried, not wanting to believe that his own lack of confidence weakened him.

It was hours later that he gave up and turned away. The plain was empty, their troops either captive or gone. David could only pray that Kastinoe still lived. Morgo led him to a boulder, sat him down next to Jendyfi, and handed him a tin mug of cold tea and a slab of cheese and bread.

The elven man looked deeply at him. "Those

giants . . ." Morgo said. "Be moving so strange and unnatural—jerky . . ."

"Yes," said Jendyfi. "Not like the ogres."

Morgo said, "I think the giants be made quickly—in a rush."

"Stiff as puppets," Jendyfi said. "They left the plain twisting, as if . . ."

"As if they be weak," Morgo said. "Created quickly, may be such beasts cannot be holding life very long. Now at dusk we be putting our horses in that pasture up there." He nodded toward a small band of fenced horses. "I be coming back for my mount tonight—I be leaving you with the tanner, at Carthen. He be trusted."

"But I . . ." David began.

"You will wait," Morgo said. "If the king be captured, your medallion be the only power left. You not be following me. We be needing you here, waiting, David Shepherd."

"But the king . . ."

"You remain here in safety as Kastinoe instructed me before ever we be leaving Caer Kastinoe. You be waiting until we learn what has happened—until I come for you. I be returning to Caer Kastinoe to bring fresh troops, and to send word again to the armies of the North. May be the messengers Kastinoe sent did not get through."

"But if Kastinoe dies there . . ."

135

"If Kastinoe dies, he be leaving no heir to rule Meryn. Only a king bearing the medallion would be strong enough." Morgo gave David a steady, meaningful look that turned David cold.

Had Kastinoe meant that he would be the next king? He was frozen with disbelief. And a sharp fear filled him that he would not see his family again.

He had held, all this time, the hope that he would somehow get home.

Jendyfi took his hand. He looked at her a long time, clinging with desperation to her strong, steady gaze.

They waited all day. At dusk they loosed the horses in the pasture, and buried the saddles and bridles in a deep hole covered with leaves. It was starting to grow dark when they went on, toward the village.

Carthen was built along the river. They stood in the forest looking out at its cobbled streets and stone houses. The sky was nearly dark. They could hear ducks gabbling and see folk hurrying along the narrow streets, going home to supper. They watched a small boy driving a herd of sheep down from a high pasture; Jendyfi said, "I'm so hungry I could eat one of those lambs alive." They were cold, hurting from their wounds. Not until the streets seemed empty did they move on into the town.

The main street was lined with shops, their

windows dark, though the living quarters above were lighted, their candlelight showing balconies crowded with crates of chickens and potted plants and cages of birds.

At the street corners, lanterns hanging from poles lit the shops of potters and a smith, a winemaker, a weaver. The town smelled of wood fires. They passed a shoemaker, a silversmith. At the far edge of the village they entered into a stink so bad that David and Jendyfi gagged.

"The tanner," Morgo said, and David thought of bloody animal skins growing ripe in the sun.

"You will get used to the smell," said Morgo. "It is the raw hides, but also the tanning solution—urine and chicken dung." He led them through the dark tannery yard and in the back door of a two-story brick building. He seemed to know the place well, for he found a lantern at once. When it was lit, David could see that the bottom floor of the building was a goat barn. Some of the goats woke and bleated at them. Morgo left them there, climbing a narrow stair beside the stalls to the living quarters above.

In a few minutes he returned with the tanner, an elven man, small and tightly made, as brown and leathery as if he had tried the tanning on himself.

"I am Coridun. You can clean out a goat stall and put in fresh straw for your beds. Here." He handed them a plate of dark bread and cold roasted goat meat, and a jug of milk.

"You will have chores here. Children are expected to work in this town. Any who do not are suspect. I will say you are new apprentices sent out from Caer Kastinoe."

Morgo hugged them and left. He didn't tell them not to be afraid or not to worry.

All their hope for gathering new troops lay with Morgo now.

Coridun went back upstairs. David and Jendyfi ate ravenously, made their straw beds, and fell into them half asleep. It seemed only minutes until Coridun was shouting to wake them; David stared up sleepily at dawn through the open barn door. He rose, pulled on his shoes, and went out.

In the tannery yard a boy was already bent over logs, scraping with a knife at a raw animal skin. Another boy, younger, slipped away into a shed. There were wooden vats in the yard, a pile of hides, some barrels, several piles of manure. It still smelled. Coridun set David to work sweeping up white membrane and hair scraped from the hides.

"Excellent," he said, when he saw that David knew how to use a broom and a flat-nosed shovel. "Put it all in that tub, so the dogs can't get it. The hair makes them vomit." Two big, ugly dogs with scruffy coats were lounging at the edge of the yard, scowling at David with expressions he didn't much like.

Jendyfi stood quietly waiting for Coridun's directions.

"Do you know how to care for goats, girl?"

"Oh yes!" She sounded so relieved, David had to smile.

"You will help my wife. If you are sufficiently skilled, you can take over the herd. She is far along with child, not feeling well. She says the smell of the yard bothers her."

David didn't see Jendyfi again until evening, when he went to wash in a wooden tub behind the goat cellar. He scrubbed, dried himself on a patched towel, and found Jendyfi in the barn mucking out stalls. The milk goats looked at him with jewel-eyed interest, bleating behind their barred doors. After the smell of the tannery, the smell of goat was sweet. "The apprentices sleep there," Jendyfi said, indicating the next stall. "Come on, Chira has supper ready."

David followed her up the narrow stairs. The room above spanned the house from front to back, under heavy, rough beams. The apprentices were already seated at the long trestle table, with the tanner and his very pregnant wife and four stair-step children. The children stared at them round eyed, but didn't speak. The smaller apprentice boy, Siarl, kept his head bent, watching his plate. He had hardly spoken to David all day.

The meal was roasted goat meat and some kind of boiled roots with onions. No one talked much, except to ask for seconds. Chira reached over her protruding stomach to cut up the meat for the smallest child. She was a pale woman and moved slowly. She gave David a dull smile that did little to push back the lines of boredom or discomfort. Coridun said, "The word in town is that when King Kastinoe's armies were defeated, Kastinoe was captured. And that the Company of Haun and the wyverlyn were captured with him."

David could eat no more.

When the meal was finished, he and Jendyfi cleared up the dishes. When they were alone in the kitchen, she said, "He is alive, David."

He nodded, not trusting himself to speak.

They washed the dishes in a metal tub, heating the water on the woodstove, both thinking of the king and of the Company and Haun.

Alone in their stall, Jendyfi said, "Do you think it's true? All of them captive?"

"We have to figure out how to help them."

"We must wait for Morgo, as he told you."

He didn't answer. He needed to do more than wait.

He could hear Jendyfi wriggling deeper into the straw. In the next stall, young Siarl cried out suddenly as if he was dreaming, and that made the goats stir and bleat. David waited impatiently for those around him to sleep. His fears for Kastinoe seemed worse in the dark.

chapter 15

When at last Jendyfi slept, David held the medallion tight in his closed fist, trying to see Kastinoe and the Company. He tried for a very long time. No vision came; but suddenly his surroundings changed—he seemed no longer in the stall. The wind blew cold around him, he sped running through the night; running not like a boy but like a beast—as if he were the hound, racing with long, leaping strides.

He drank the wind as the hound did, scenting a hundred smells: small beasts, earth, water; felt every change in the wind, every stone beneath his pads, heard every frightened scuttling of creatures fleeing from him through the dark. Something of himself had gone with Bran; something of his own spirit sped across the plain. Not until they reached the Undercity and were circling the hills did he try to direct the hound. *Find the king! Find Kastinoe!* He wanted to go underground into the city, but Bran veered away from the three caves, David could not control him, could only feel his muscles tighten as he turned.

Find the king!

Bran circled the hills, pausing at the edge of a narrow canyon cut across the plain. David could see its flat walls near the surface, but could see nothing deep down, only blackness. He started to shout, but woke suddenly, lay staring around the shadowed stall. Outside, the yard dogs were barking with rage and fear.

He sat up, throwing back straw.

It was barely light. He heard, beneath the yard dogs' hysterical barking, someone weeping. Jendyfi?

No, Jendyfi was already gone—milking, he supposed; he could hear buckets clanging. And this was a boy crying, a young boy. He sat up, listening. When the child didn't stop crying, he got up.

He passed Jendyfi milking in a far corner of the barn. She shook her head. "I went to them, but they ignored me. I didn't want to press—he was crying so hard."

David pushed into the boys' stall.

Siarl lay belly down in the straw, tense and hunched, bawling. The older boy, Lefi, sat against the wall, watching him. David looked them over.

"What did you do to him?"

"Nothing. Didn't touch him."

"What's the matter with him?"

"Had a nightmare. Has them a lot."

"What about? He's your brother, isn't he?"

"No. I never saw him before he came here."

David leaned against the wall. "What kind of nightmare?"

"I don't know. He never remembers them. They always make him cry." The barn was growing light. Jendyfi's bucket banged. David knelt beside Siarl.

"It's all right. It was only a dream, a bad dream." He looked up at Lefi.

"Where did he live before he came here?"

"I don't know. The street, like me." Lefi rose indifferently, pulled on his pants, and went to wash.

The next night Bran came to David, a dense, huge blackness outside the stall, then slipping silently in beside him. David knelt up on his blanket, watching the hound's gleaming eyes. Bran towered over him, pressing against him, leaning down to rest his broad muzzle on David's shoulder. Excited by Bran's wildness, David hugged Bran's shaggy neck, laid his cheek against the hound's hard-muscled side and rough coat, felt Bran's breath hot and ragged against his throat.

"Where is the king?" David whispered. "Take me to Kastinoe."

Bran did not respond, but growled again, low and menacing, then lay down beside him, a mountain of warmth.

David slept against Bran's shoulder, surprised that the hound would stay; and secure in Bran's fierce presence. But in the morning his hound was gone.

The barn floor, outside the stall, was marked with Bran's broad pawprints deep in the soft dirt.

That morning the little apprentice looked at David differently, glancing at him and down again quickly, his black hair falling to hide his face. And that morning Chira hid David and Jendyfi suddenly when a wagon came into the yard, dragging them hastily up the stairs to her bedroom. "Don't make a sound. Here, take this knife. Stay until I come for you!"

They heard low, muffled voices in the yard. After the wagon left, there was silence for some time before Chira came to get them.

"What was it?" Jendyfi said.

"They were looking for you—two men. If they come again and you cannot hide, run—up into the woods."

That night, in the small hours, David woke to see Bran in the stall again. But this time young Siarl was beside him.

Siarl's arms were around the hound's neck, and even when Bran growled, staring toward the door, the little boy clung unafraid. David rose, amazed. Siarl didn't move. Bran growled again, and there was another noise in the barn. David went out into the dark barn and searched, but there was no one there. When he returned, Bran stared at him for a moment, raised a wail that set the goats thrashing and the yard dogs howling, then pulled away from Siarl and vanished into shadow.

Siarl turned to go to bed, but David pulled him back, kneeling beside the little boy, trying to see his face. "What made you go to the hound? Why didn't it frighten you?"

"Why would it frighten me? It is just a big dog."

"Who are you? Where do you come from?"

"I am Siarl. I am no one. I come from the street—I am a street child." The look behind Siarl's eyes was closed, blank and ungiving.

David touched Siarl's black hair. "Jendyfi found a jar of black dye today. Do you dye your hair?"

Siarl nodded. "They want me, on the streets— a pale-haired boy."

"Want you for what?"

146

"For stealing."

David asked no more—he thought it would do no good. And his questions were forgotten the next morning when another wagon turned into the tannery yard and driving it was the woman from the palace kitchen—Prudd! At the sight of her, he backed into the shadows among a pile of barrels, his heart pounding. Jendyfi was with the goats. He couldn't reach her without Prudd seeing him.

Prudd seemed to know Chira, who had come into the yard. Prudd's voice was harsh, demanding. "I want the boy."

"Which boy?" Chira sounded tired.

"The boy who can bring the hound."

"What hound? We have only common yard dogs, not hunting hounds. What—?"

"The black hound! Don't play stupid with me, Chira!"

"What black hound? I don't understand what you're talking about. Can't you make sense?"

"Kastinoe's hound—the hound of power! I said don't play stupid with me!"

"Do you mean the hound of the medallion? What would I know about that? How could some boy have anything to do with that?"

"The hound runs. The beast has been seen coming from the tannery. Where is the boy? I want him."

Chira sighed with exasperation. "We have

boys—dull drudges—in the tannery. Take any you want. It's all I can do to get meals on the table, I have no time to look after little boys."

Prudd grabbed Chira by the shoulders. "You have the boy, and I want him."

"Take whatever boy you wish. Drudge children. Not one of them capable of a sensible thought. Lazy—they can hardly sweep the goat stalls properly."

"The king is our prisoner," said Prudd.

"So?"

"If we don't get the boy, Kastinoe dies. You can . . ."

Prudd's voice stopped, David heard footsteps, but before he could run the thin woman loomed over him, grabbing him, her fingers digging like spikes. He hit her hard; she fell, but was up again, moving like a fighter, twisting his arm behind him, strong as a man.

"No!" he shouted. And Bran was there, leaping at Prudd, knocking her down, snarling over her, tensed to kill. Blood spilled down Prudd's throat, she struggled under the hound's weight. Bran had not depended on fear to drive her back, and that made David know how dangerous she was. Bran reached again . . .

And vanished.

David could not bring him back.

Balcher's power had protected her, had weakened the hound. Struck with terror, David

cursed his own helplessness against the man—
and against the Degra, who surely helped
Balcher. He had a sudden, clear sense of the Degra's cruel powers, which the medallions were
made to defeat. But then, looking at the woman,
who seemed frail now, sprawled before him
bleeding and glancing up at him with pleading
eyes, he felt pity.

The next moment Prudd lurched up from the
dirt, all evil returned to her face, reaching for
him, chilling him so badly he abandoned dignity
and ran.

chapter 16

David found Jendyfi feeding the goats and pulled her away. "It's Prudd out there—come on!" They retrieved their packs and made for the back door.

But Siarl stood blocking them. As David pushed by, the little boy grabbed his arm.

"Take me with you."

As David started to thrust him aside, Siarl's eyes spoke all that was needed: fear, and something more that made David know he couldn't leave this child. "Come on."

They ran ducking low, through tall weeds across the back field, slid under the fence, and pushed between trees lining the river, then along the bank, sinking in wet moss. When Prudd's voice shouted from the tannery, in desperation they plunged into the black water, holding their packs high.

Siarl swam quick as a fish, the first across and out onto the opposite bank, crawling through weeds into the woods. David and Jendyfi followed, squeezing water out of their clothes, climbing through the steep, dense woods, pushing through vine-tangled thickets, trying to be quiet.

When they were far away, they let themselves rest, sharing out some of the dried meat and bread from the packs, and drinking sparingly from David's flask. Jendyfi spied a few fruits and climbed the thick, twisting tree.

She brought down a dozen small, dry-looking fruits that, when bitten, filled their mouths with a cool, sweet juice. "The last ones," she said. "Likely the birds got the rest." They ate crouching among the thick brush, trapped by the heavy stillness, then went on.

In the hot afternoon insects began to buzz. Sweat ran from their hair into their faces, and little flies flew into it and stuck. Every movement of a bird or a small animal turned them rigid. Below them lay the village, and they could see men searching for them.

Siarl said, "Did Prudd see me, back there?"

"I don't think so," David said. "Do you know her? Where did you know her?"

Siarl didn't answer.

"Come on, Siarl. Who would we tell? We're running from her, too."

"She was—she comes from the Undercity," Siarl said, his voice flat.

"Then so do you?" David said, surprised. "Tell us."

"I—lived in the Undercity until a year ago. Some—some slaves escaped and took me with them. In the Undercity Prudd—Prudd was our keeper. She beat us, and hurt us if we didn't do as she said. Sometimes—the Degra made bets on which of us could stand up to her the longest, before we begged her to stop."

David was shocked. He put his arm around Siarl, held the little boy close. "How did you get away?"

"Through a supply tunnel."

"Which one? I could see three tunnels."

"On—on the right, as you look at the hills."

Jendyfi reached to take Siarl's hands, turned them over, touching his palms. "Your hands aren't callused, Siarl. The slaves of the Undercity have deep, thick calluses."

"We didn't work the mines. They kept us apart in a separate cave. Nine of us, nine boys."

"Why? Why would they do that? What work did you do?"

"I don't know why. They taught us things, they said that was our work."

"If you were in the Undercity, how did you learn to swim?" Jendyfi said.

"There was an underground river to drink

from. There were bars under the water so we couldn't swim away. They taught us, over and over, how good the Degra are, and how they would save Meryn."

Jendyfi said, "Did you believe them?"

"Sometimes they made us believe them. They take your mind away. They made us believe that something wonderful would happen, that they were gods and that they loved us—that our lives would be wonderful someday.

"But then when we didn't do what they wanted, Prudd would beat us. Or she would take us down into the black tunnels. She threatened to leave us there in the dark to die of hunger and thirst."

David said, "Why did they keep you apart? Were you different somehow?"

"I don't know why. How could we be different?"

"Did you live there all your life? Do you remember anything before?"

"I—I don't remember." Siarl pulled away from David and pushed against Jendyfi; she gathered him in.

David felt Siarl's pain deeply. But he wanted answers. "What do you remember before the Undercity? Were you always there? Do you remember something before it?"

"I don't know."

"Try. Try to remember."

The little boy whimpered.

"Please try," David said carefully.

"I—sometimes. Sometimes . . . a woman holding me, rocking me."

"Your mother?"

"I don't know."

"Where? Where was it?"

"A big room with stone walls and a fire."

"What else? What did she look like? What color was her hair?"

"I don't remember—I don't know."

"Why did they keep you nine apart from the others?"

"They said we would have special work someday."

"Of the nine, did they treat *you* any different from the others?"

"No." The little boy sighed.

"Tell us more about the tunnels," David said. "Tell us everything you can."

"They put prisoners there to die of thirst and hunger. Even if they could escape, there is only one way out of the tunnels—through the cave of the Chimotaur. The beast would kill them, tear them apart. No one," Siarl said, swallowing, "could kill the Chimotaur.

"Sometimes they brought it up through a gate into the city, all chained, and led it through the streets to sniff out traitors. It is a huge man with a bull's head and the tail of a dragon."

Jendyfi said, "The Degra made the Chimotaur with their dark powers and their knives. There are minotaurs in the far mountains and harmless chimera. The Degra put them together, with their dark magic."

Siarl said, "Sometimes the Degra guards made us stand at the edge of a narrow chasm so we could see the Chimotaur deep down and hear it roaring."

David stared at him. The cleft—the black cleft that Bran had shown him.

"If a slave tried to escape, they threw him into the cleft. They made us watch the Chimotaur kill him."

David said, "Would they put the captured king there?"

"I expect so."

"But the power of his medallion . . ." Jendyfi began.

"Maybe it could keep the Chimotaur away," Siarl said. "Except—for how long? He'd get weak, with no food or water—and he wouldn't dare sleep. He couldn't last." He shrugged, turned away. "The Chimotaur would kill him."

"How many ways into the cave of the Chimotaur?" David said.

"Two. The long way through the dark caves and the short tunnel where they can bring the Chimotaur out. Both open from the main entrance to the city."

"Where is the shorter tunnel?"

"On the far left—there's an iron gate inside."

"Locked?"

"There's a lock the Chimotaur can't open. You have to reach into a deep cylinder and press something—one of the slaves told me."

Evening came to the woods quickly. They felt hidden by the darkness, but threatened, too. In the light of the rising moon they found the pasture where they had left their mounts. The sight of the little band of horses cheered them. They were almost to the fence when they were grabbed from behind. A man held David, nearly breaking his ribs, a hand across his eyes as David fought and kicked. They were thrown over shoulders like bundles, slammed into trees and jabbed by branches as their captors moved fast through the woods, heading downhill. When David called Bran, the man hit him, hard. Bran did not come. David twisted, hitting him in the head, and felt the slick bald scalp and the scar snaking across.

Terrified, relief swept him as he saw a black hound leaping at him through blackness—but it was Balcher's hound, his teeth slashing his ankle, his claws raking at his dangling legs. He tried to choke Balcher, kicking him in the belly and groin. When Balcher grunted and doubled over, David broke free and hit the ground running.

Something crashed behind him. Bran? He heard a branch break, heard Balcher swear, then heard hounds fighting. Bran must be there, holding Balcher's hound back. He headed in the direction of the pasture, running hard, tripping, dodging branches. The snarling of the battling hounds grew faint. Ahead, the trees parted against the night sky. He prayed that clearing was the pasture.

He found the pasture fence and slipped under it. There was only silence behind him.

As he searched for the place Morgo had buried the saddles, he heard Prudd shouting far off, "Lock them up! Perhaps we'll have a use for the boy." Puzzled, terrified for Jendyfi and Siarl, he found the saddles and dug one free, with a bridle.

He made himself approach the horses slowly, as Morgo had shown him. He saw Jendyfi's white mare, hoped the gray shape was the gelding he knew. He pulled handfuls of seeds from the tall grass; dropping them into a fold of his leather tunic, and shaking them, he made them rattle like grain in a feed bag. Thus he approached the horses, walking easy.

He slipped the bridle on the gelding as the good beast nuzzled the seeds. He saddled him, found the gate, and was soon through and astride. As he made his way down the hill, he heard galloping horses ahead, a whip crack. He kicked the gelding into a run; soon a wagon loomed ahead. In the light of its swinging lantern he could see the cage it carried, with Jendyfi and Siarl inside, gripping the bars. The cart horses swerved under Balcher's whip, lunging and jerking the wagon, heading for the Undercity. David drew close, studying the heavy, barred door and swinging lock, reaching to touch the bars.

"Get away!" Jendyfi hissed. "It's you they want. We're— I think we're bait. Get away, David!"

David moved away, looking ahead to the Undercity; then he leaned low and kicked the gelding hard.

As he passed Balcher, the man laughed. "That's it, boy. Hurry on to the Undercity! Hurry to the Degra, where your hound can run for us!"

"Never!" David shouted, and pushed his horse on, thinking only of the king, of reaching him before Balcher did. Yet, in the Undercity, surrounded by the Degra, what defense would he have against Balcher?

Fear of that dark city and the thousands of Degra made him falter and want to turn back, and, again, a chilling sense of defeat sapped his power. The good gelding pounded on across the plain, David clinging and uncertain, the wagon thundering close behind.

He was almost to the hills when something

made him look back: The moon was higher, and against the sky was a pale, moving dust cloud. At its base ran a long line of galloping horse soldiers speeding for the Undercity—the troops from Caer Kastinoe. He stood in the saddle wanting to shout, then sped on, heartened. Balcher, having seen them, swerved the wagon toward a tunnel in the hills.

Soon the army was passing David far to the left. The wagon had disappeared. Ahead, Degra armies were boiling up out of the Undercity, thousands of ogres and mounted Degra troops, and droowgs swarming into the moonlit sky.

chapter 17

Arrows flew close to David. Balcher's wagon careened out of the mountain as Kastinoe's troops pounded toward the hills, and endless Degra warriors thundered out of the Undercity straight at them. Suddenly Balcher pulled his horses to a rearing halt. Standing atop the wagon, he raised his arms high, held high the third medallion: Balcher's hound exploded into Kastinoe's troops. Horses reared screaming and fell in panic, throwing their riders to be slashed by the running beast.

David turned the gelding away, riding for the cleft: He must find Kastinoe. But Balcher's hound was after him, knocking him from the saddle at the edge of the chasm; he fell sprawled on the lip of the deep gorge.

Standing over him, the hound looked past him

down into the empty dark. David turned to look down, his cheek brushing pebbles into space.

The wall dropped away sheer and smooth, and far below a brown, turgid river ran. He saw the prisoners then, tied against the cliff wall.

Llellwyn's red cloak flickered in a small breeze that must come off the river. Haun's head had been pulled back against the wall by ropes, his wings bound to his body. The king, shackled to the cliff, faced the Chimotaur.

The beast was huge, rocking back and forth on heavy legs, reaching for Kastinoe; a beast twice the size of Haun, its shaggy bull's head swinging, its dragon tail sliding over the stones. It moved smoothly, pressing toward the king. It could not reach him; the power of Kastinoe's medallion held it away.

But Kastinoe only held it; he could not escape it. David looked back at Balcher's hound. He snarled, reaching for his throat. David grabbed his mouth, twisting, his fingers holding his teeth. Sceolan bowed his neck, jerking away. Then his mouth came over David's face.

But something made him stop. He didn't tear at him but backed off. When David looked into his eyes, he saw something more than rage.

"You cannot," he whispered. "In spite of Balcher, you cannot kill an heir to the medallion.

"Let Bran come to me, Sceolan. Let Bran come!"

The hound backed away, weaving his head.

"Let Bran come! You were not bred to serve evil! The medallion was not made to serve evil!"

But Balcher was too strong, Balcher and the Degra together too strong. Sceolan would not kill him, but Sceolan would not help him. David reached to touch Sceolan's shaggy shoulder, then heard a sound behind him. Hands grabbed his shoulders; he was lifted, held out over the edge of the chasm, over empty space.

"Look down," Balcher hissed, chuckling. "Look down, David Shepherd!" David stared down at dropping space.

"Now, David Shepherd! Now you will join with me, now! You have no choice. You will join me or you will die down there smashed against the stones."

"I *won't* join you!"

"Bring the child," Balcher shouted. David twisted around to see Prudd dragging Siarl. She pulled the little boy to the edge, held him over. Siarl fought, white and silent.

David grabbed Balcher's legs and locked his arms around them. When Balcher hit him, David took the pain, gritting his teeth, hanging on.

"If we die, Balcher, you die!" He clung, imagining the fall. "Where is your hound, Balcher? He's only a shadow now! Look—a shadow! You've lost your power over him! The hound was bred for good, not evil! He cannot hold forever to evil! You're losing him!"

A cold, sure strength filled David. "You couldn't take the king's medallion! You couldn't take Kastinoe's medallion even when you chained him! Nor can you take mine! You can't stop our power! Together we will defeat you! Your own hound will turn against you, Balcher. With the three hounds we will defeat you!"

"You're wrong, boy. It is Kastinoe's power that is weakening. He holds the Chimotaur at bay, nothing more. He does not hold the Degra army from battle now. Listen to your soldiers scream as the Undercity troops slaughter them!

"Your king might save himself from the Chimotaur. Or he might save his armies. But Kastinoe cannot do both. He has not the power to do both."

"He does now! There are two medallions now!"

Balcher's eyes were filled with amusement. "*You* can't help Kastinoe! You can't even help yourself." He shook David, slid one hand away, let David dangle by his collar and by David's grip on Balcher's legs.

"You'd best join me while you still can, boy. If you want to live." Balcher unsheathed his knife, poising the blade over David's wrist. "I can easily cut you loose from me."

"If you're so powerful, Balcher, why *do* you need *me*? Why *are* you trying so hard to make me join you?"

Balcher's eyes hardened.

"If *I* don't help you, Balcher, you can't win! Your medallion and the king's remain in balance. I can join Kastinoe or I can join you. I am the deciding force."

Balcher snatched at David's medallion, jerking it off. David lunged, clutching Balcher; they fell on the edge, struggling, the medallion lost between them—there, beneath Balcher's knee! Siarl and Prudd scrambled for it, and as Siarl snatched it up, Prudd's fist smashed down on Siarl's neck; then Prudd and Siarl were over the edge, falling—David lunged for Siarl, felt only air.

Siarl fell, the medallion flashing in his hand, Prudd clinging to him, falling with him. David was half over, reaching into empty space, felt himself jerked back, Jendyfi gripping his legs. He watched Siarl spinning down and down, dragged against Prudd. . . .

The fall seemed to take forever, silent in the wind. Then, far below, the water rose in a soundless splash.

They were gone.

Siarl—gone . . . the medallion gone.

David rolled away, sick. Gone, poor Siarl—and the power of the medallion gone. Balcher had won, the Degra would enslave Meryn now. Kastinoe would die.

Balcher fought Jendyfi, trying insanely to throw her over too, shouting, *"Gone! The medallion—gone!"* He lunged for David. *"Nothing—you're worth nothing now! All my effort—all . . ."*

David hit him hard, kicked him as he fell, grabbed Jendyfi; they ran.

chapter 18

They ran toward the tunnels dodging charging horses as more Degra troops stormed out. "The left tunnel!" David shouted, swerving. They fled down into darkness, listening for pounding behind them. Their running footsteps echoed against dark walls. The tunnel smelled of wet stone.

They crashed into the gate, seeking frantically for a lock. David found a long cylinder and reached in, pressing something deep inside. The gate swung open. Ahead, they heard the thundering roars of the Chimotaur.

The tunnel was slippery; in some places they ran through water. Far ahead a smear of dim light shone, and soon the beast's bellowing nearly deafened them. They slowed, joining hands.

Around a curve, in sudden light, the cleft

opened, and there was the grotto of the Chimotaur, shaken with the beast's thundering
roars. The man-beast paced not twenty feet from
them, its snaking tail thrashing heavily across
the cavern floor as it fought the barrier of the
king's power. Bawling, it thrust its shoulders
toward Kastinoe, trying to breech that invisible
wall. David felt for his knife, and thought he
might as well use a toothpick against the monster.

The king and warriors, tied against the wall,
did not turn to look at David and Jendyfi, but
glancing their way, their eyes lit with hope. The
king stood tall, the line of his jaw stubborn, the
muscled roll of his shoulders ungiving. Starved
and surely sick from his dark, swollen wounds,
he still wielded the medallion's power. David
pressed against the side of the arch, watching
him, stricken with Kastinoe's stubborn, unbend-
ing will. Then he followed Jendyfi's gaze upward,
examining the curving stone arch above him.

"There's a lip along it," Jendyfi said. "Look—
where the edging row of stones juts out."

He reached to feel the wide lip that ran from
the floor up over the arch. "I can climb that. Can
you distract the Chimotaur?"

"Yes."

David looked deeply at her, wondering if they
would die here. "Let's untie Haun and the men."

They moved through shadows toward the

prisoners. David began to untie Morgo, as Jendyfi slipped past him to work on Glud.

The knots were hard, tangled; it seemed to take forever. The Chimotaur roared and thundered, watching them. Who knew whether it was smart enough to understand what they were doing. At last they had two prisoners free; they freed the king; soon all the men were untied. Glud moved slowly, to unchain the wyverlyn.

David slipped back through the shadows, his heart pounding as the Chimotaur turned to watch him, and climbed the jutting arch. Behind him, the beast's hooves scraped the stone floor. As he reached the top, Jendyfi shouted at the Chimotaur, waved her arms, and ran in front of it. It swung to charge her; she dodged, shouted again, and the warriors leaped for it, yelling, running in every direction. It lunged at one, then another as they led it close to David.

But it swung by him too fast, charging Arean. Arean barely dodged it, doubled back, and ran through the arch; the beast followed, again swinging close to David, its head nearly grazing him: He leaped, straddling its shoulder, and thrust the knife into its throat.

It gurgled, faltered beneath him. As it careened, falling, he felt a sudden terrible pity for the huge man-beast. And then, recovering, carried by its frenzy, it ran blindly at the warriors, David clinging. Haun leaped on it in an explosion of wings, and as David jumped free, Haun drove the Chimotaur smashing against the wall.

The beast thrashed, clutching at the wall with its human arms, gave a last shudder and a hoarse roar, and lay still.

The shock of pity held them all. The beast had been terrible and magnificent.

For David, the fear that had waned and risen within him now was gone altogether. He felt changed, older, finished with a last childish uncertainty. He looked steadily at Kastinoe, deeply aware of the strength that had lifted this man from near-death and defeat.

The warriors prodded the Chimotaur to be sure it was dead; then king and warriors sped for the river, knelt, and drank greedily.

When at last Morgo lifted his streaming face, he was grinning broadly. "Oh, that be grand water. That be the first water in three days."

Now that the cave was quiet, they could hear the cries of battle careening down at them between the canyon walls. The warriors ran for the passage; but the king stopped suddenly and turned back, staring downriver.

The river ran turgid and brown, the bank on the far side undercut, both shores slick with mud. Where Kastinoe was looking, a lump of mud moved.

A muddy hand moved, then a small muddy arm, a child's arm.

They raced down through the mud, reached him, scooped mud away from the little boy's face, wiped mud from his eyes and nose and from inside his mouth. David lifted him. How frail the child felt, and ice cold. Jendyfi scooped up river water and began to wash the mud from his face, but Siarl pulled away from her, and fumbled for something in his pocket.

He shoved his fist at David and opened his hand. David stared, then clutched wildly at the shine of gold.

He wiped mud from the medallion. As he slipped the chain over his head, light from the river caught the gold disc, making it burn like a sun.

The warriors stood looking from one medallion to the other. Then, standing calf deep in the mud of the Undercity river, they all looked at Siarl, at this little boy who had, against all odds, saved himself and saved a Medallion of the Black Hound. One, then another of the warriors reached to touch him, and Haun gave the little boy a long lick up his arm and cheek.

The sounds of battle stirred them; they roused themselves and made for the tunnel. David, glancing at Kastinoe, at the strong face of this determined and powerful man, vowed that now, together, they would defeat Balcher.

chapter 19

They broke out of the tunnel, the warriors grabbing weapons from dead men; Haun and Llellwyn leaped skyward shouting a challenge. Kastinoe stood still, motioning David near him; Siarl followed, clinging to David's hand. Fighting surrounded them; the three stood, incredibly small and vulnerable amidst the battle. The king lifted his medallion, held it high: The medallion of Tuiren shone bright against the rising sun, and Kastinoe called Tuiren and David called to Bran. Wildly the two hounds burst into battle, leaping up at hard-riding Degra warriors.

But atop the mountain Balcher held his medallion reflecting red from the sunrise, reflecting blood; and the hound Sceolan burst alive on the mountain, leaping and roaring down the crags toward Bran and Tuiren. The two turned, left the battle to face him; charging up the mountain.

Halfway up, among sliding stones, the two hounds met the one. There on the mountain, exploding with wild Celtic magic, two hounds battled one.

Balcher's hound drew back, groveling before the two others. In his submission was something strange, not beaten, yet no longer fierce. Something new seemed to have awakened within Sceolan; or something long lost. His lowered, wagging tail, his alert watchfulness, seemed gestures almost of amazement.

"Now," said the king softly. "Now—call all of Mac Cumhal's hounds, David. Help me call the pack."

They came like blown leaves swirling out of nowhere, raging and snarling, dozens of great dark beasts taking the battlefield in long leaps, following Tuiren as she charged, and spun, and charged again. Before them confused troops fell from plunging horses, and fear-struck Degra warriors fled for the Undercity.

"Now!" cried Kastinoe. "Now!" And Bran and Tuiren swung around, leaving the victorious pack, leaping up the mountain to dispatch Balcher. Though David knew the man as coldly evil, now suddenly, at his death, David was sickened.

*　　*　　*

The two hounds turned from Balcher's body and came quietly to David and the king. But there were not two hounds. There were three. They pressed at David, at Kastinoe—and at Siarl. The hound of Balcher pressed at Siarl, smiling into the little boy's face.

David saw mud smeared on Kastinoe's tunic where Siarl stood close to him. He saw Siarl's hair where mud had brushed away, leaving it no longer black but washed blond by the river.

Kastinoe put his hand on Siarl's muddy shoulder. The third hound, taller than Siarl, was quietly licking Siarl's cheek, his tail wagging. Kastinoe touched the hound lightly, then knelt before Siarl, holding the child's shoulders, looking deeply into the little boy's face.

He looked at Siarl for a very long time, at the boy's pale hair, at his eyes. The king took Siarl's hands in his own, turning them over, examining their shape. He touched Siarl's ears, scraping the mud away to look at ears and neck and chin.

He looked into Siarl's eyes and smiled. Then Kastinoe rose, and when he spoke, his voice was gruff. "Go to the bald man who lies dead on the mountain. Take the medallion from his body."

Siarl looked up at the king with wide eyes, then turned away toward the mountain.

When Siarl had climbed and returned, and

stood, again, before the king, holding the golden disc, Kastinoe took it from him. Kastinoe was still, looking down at the child a moment. Then the king dropped the chain around Siarl's neck— just as, in another world, David's father had placed his medallion.

"Kastin," the king said, seeing the confusion in the little boy's eyes. "You are Kastin, muddy and heroic and beautiful. Do you remember that you are my son?"

"I—I . . . How could it be? How could you know such a thing?"

"No one can wear a Medallion of the Black Hound save one born to it. No one but such an heir can touch a medallion.

"And no one," said the king, "but the son of the queen of Meryn could have such eyes as yours. I know your mother's look." And Kastinoe scooped the child up against his broad chest and held him tight.

David had turned away from father and son, leaving them alone. Kastinoe's warriors were busy with the wounded, and with injured horses. Jendyfi stood with her back to David, crying.

He put his arm around her. "What? What's the matter?"

She looked up at him, all watery. "Just . . ." She glanced toward the king. "Just—that they are so happy!" She cried harder, into his shoulder. But soon she wiped her eyes and grinned at him. "Just—that they found each other, that they will both be happy now." She wiped her eyes again and hugged him.

When Haun returned from chasing the last droowgs, he was followed by four wyverlyns smacking and licking their whiskers; a sleek gray female flew beside him. "Fine droowgs!" Haun shouted, purring. "Fine hunters we are! Grand hunters!" He settled contentedly against the mountain close beside the gray wyverlyn, their wings folded over each other. Morgo looked at Llellwyn and winked. "May be, two companies of wyverlyn be joining."

"May be," said Llellwyn.

Soon, released slaves began to come up out of the Undercity in little frightened bands. They were escorted by Kastinoe's soldiers, but out on the open plain, under empty sky, they seemed alarmed, huddling together, would look at no one, talk to no one. Many tried to turn back into the dark small spaces that were all they knew. The soldiers made a camp for them, guiding them to it kindly, gathering wood for warming fires, sharing out their own blankets and food. David wondered if these poor, terrified men and women would ever shake loose the crippling done to them by the Degra and grow into strong, free folk.

Through all the mopping up, the king kept Siarl close. David watched Kastinoe and the small prince together, and was comforted by a strong sense of completeness.

Siarl might have died in that river: Kastinoe and his son might have been brought together in the cleft and parted again, neither knowing who the other was.

Now, with the two medallions together, the king and his son would destroy the remaining small camps of Degra and free Meryn forever.

Or will it be three medallions? David thought.

Will I be a part of Meryn for the rest of my life? He looked across at Jendyfi and knew it would be all right. He could not imagine being without her. Exhaustion filled him now, and home seemed unreal and remote.

Siarl was saying, ". . . because it was Prudd that saved me. I fell on top of her—she couldn't swim. She nearly drowned me, fighting to stay afloat. I hit her until she let go. You didn't see that," he said to his father. "We were too far downriver."

Morgo said, "We be seeing you fall, young prince. That Prudd woman, she be hanging on to you pretty hard—the two of you tumbling like two fighting birds tangled together."

David looked up the mountain to where Balcher had so recently stood; he was feeling light-headed, he guessed he needed sleep. As he turned, he saw Jendyfi's startled face, saw Morgo reach out to him, shocked. He grabbed for Morgo's hand but touched only air. Everyone was fading. *"No!"* he shouted. His last sight of Haun was of lifted wings fading, thin as smoke. He heard Jendyfi cry, *"No! No, David . . ."* He lunged, reaching. *"Come with me . . . Jendyfi. . . ."* He felt her hands, then they were pulled from his, and he was jerked through blackness, whirled away into space. He was spinning, dizzy, cold, aching with loss, trying to will himself back to them. He thought he felt Jendyfi's hands for a moment, but it was only the whirling winds battering him, lifting him so fast his stomach felt left behind. Jendyfi—she was gone . . . *gone* . . .

He stopped spinning. The dark air brightened and stilled. He was standing on green turf; he could smell the bruised grass, feel hot sun on his back. *Gone . . . Jendyfi, gone . . .* He should hear the stands shouting. He'd have to kick the goal. . . . *He couldn't leave her, leave them all— Kastinoe, Morgo, Haun . . .* In a second he'd hear the stands shouting, have to kick the goal . . .

The stands above him were empty, silent. The soccer field was empty, he was alone.

Where was the team? Where was everyone? How long since he had been here?

He glanced down expecting to see his soccer shoes, then remembered they were gone, stared at the hand-sewn Meryn boots.

How long had he been gone?

Days?

Years?

He looked past the field to the houses.

They looked the same, a white house, then a yellow, then gray, the big oak tree on the corner with the swing hanging from it. The cars all looked the same, a blue van, a white pickup. He ran to the edge of the field, saw some drink cans thrown away, a Hershey wrapper. He turned to run home. What time was it? The sun—late afternoon. What day? Would Mom be at work? He looked toward the locker room and phone booth, felt in his pocket, knowing there wasn't any money; maybe there was a quarter left in the return slot. He started to run, stopped . . . stared . . .

Beyond the gym in the woods a black shadow raced. He watched it, shocked. *"Bran! Bran! Come back! Bran . . ."* His voice cracked like a shot in the emptiness.

The hound vanished among the trees. Then David could smell his wild scent, felt his warm breath for a moment across his neck. He touched the medallion, felt its warmth, knew Bran was with him.

When he looked up, two figures were coming

around the gym toward him. Mom—walking fast; no, running, her cap pulled off like when she was excited, lifting her hand to him, running. And Dad!

"Dad!"

They ran—he ran, shouting, plunged into their arms shouting, hugging, was lifted off the ground in Dad's bear hug.

When he could talk again, when Dad had set him down, he had a million things to tell them—to ask them. He didn't know how to start.

How could they believe him? How could they believe all that had happened? Mom touched his leather shirt and trousers—Jendyfi's clothes. His mother looked at his unfamiliar boots and sniffed his sweaty leathers, wrinkling her nose, laughing.

Dad touched the gold chain and lifted the medallion, held it. His green eyes were still and serious, questioning him.

David swallowed, didn't know where to start. "Balcher . . ." he began, "Balcher is dead. In—not in our world."

Dad didn't say anything, only studied David. He touched David's face, looking deep, his eyes filled with questions. Yet his father's gaze was beyond any hint of disbelief, took on slowly a deeper, more ancient belief than David had ever known; a solid, keen excitement.

"You're all right," Dad said at last, holding

David again, so hard he couldn't breathe.

"And you're all right," David said. "Balcher didn't— you're all right!"

"I didn't ever see him. He had already left the ship when I got there; and the medallion had disappeared. Soon after, your mother phoned, and I came home to look for you."

"How long? How long was I gone?"

"Nearly three weeks."

"How— Where did you look for me? What happened on the field—the game? Everyone must have seen—well, what *did* they see? Mom, what did you see?"

His mother frowned and hugged him again as if she couldn't get close enough. "The field where you stood got dark—just in one small place, around you, the air all swirling and dark. There wasn't any wind, the field was hot and still. But there was wind *there*, a dark, terrifying wind. I guess I was already running down the stands, because when it cleared, I was on the field. And you were gone. The team was just standing there, blank faced, staring. Then—they began to shout for you. I kept asking where you were, shaking one, then another. No one knew. I nearly punched one of the coaches, I was so upset, and then mad, that they had let something happen to you. Afterward," Mom said, "and ever since, the kids have been telling wild tales—about kidnapping—about men from space."

"And what do you say to them?" David watched his mother, comforted by her strength and wanting to laugh at the tales his friends probably dreamed up.

Mom said, "We don't argue with them. We just ask *them* questions, right back—never give a straight answer. But when you go back to school, you'll have to deal with it. I guess the best thing is just to hedge, keep them guessing—make a joke of it."

"Did—did you cry?"

"Sure I cried. But first I shouted at everyone. Later I had my hysterics alone. And after I called your father, I thought maybe you really had vanished, that you weren't kidnapped off the field. I . . . It's been pretty bad around here." She swallowed. "And the police—we had to file a Missing Persons Report. That—that made me kind of sick."

His father put his arm around her, holding her in that casual way they had, the two of them complete within themselves, yet filled, at the same time, with infinite love and caring for him.

David said, "But Dad—you guessed what happened?"

"I thought it was possible. Some of my research has hinted at things like this, but . . .

Well, it's far out, David. And I thought Balcher must be involved, and that really scared me. I thought you might be dead—that he might do that, to get the medallion." He pulled David close, the three of them making a tight little circle. "But—where is the medallion? Do you know, David? Do you know where Sceolan runs?"

"Sceolan runs—in that world, where I was—where Balcher died." There was so much to tell them, but so much he wasn't ready to talk about yet. They wouldn't push. He would take his time. David smiled. "Sceolan has a new master. The hound runs—where he belongs, I think. It's all right, Dad. I think it's all right now."